The
PLAYMAKER

The PLAYMAKER

By Curtis Kent Bishop

74796

THE STECK COMPANY • PUBLISHERS
AUSTIN, TEXAS

TO WILBUR EVANS
Who has helped make a lifetime
of sports enjoyable

Chapter One

Few things about this first scrimmage escaped Coach Forrest Denton's watchful eyes. So far, five newcomers to Belmont Junior College had made strong impressions.

Four of the new candidates had been expected to show up well in this first full-court scrimmage. Coach Denton was familiar with the high-school records of Crickett Sledge, Buster Tolar, Paul Tipton, and Eddie Moss. All had brought athletic reputations with them to Belmont.

But the fifth standout in this impromptu game for new squadmen only—Craig Townsend! Where had he played prep-school basketball? How had he managed to enroll in Belmont completely unheralded? The coaches of this junior-college conference contacted high-school prospects as zealously as did scouts for the universities and large colleges. Coach Denton, for instance, had not missed a single game of the annual state high-school tournament in fifteen years. Yet he had never heard of this Craig Townsend. The youth's eligibility card listed a year's playing experience at Compton High School. He had not earned a letter there.

Coach Denton sighed as the ten perspiring boys stopped for a short rest. Craig Townsend had height and wiriness, six-feet-three inches of it. He had not even lettered at a high school which produced only mediocre teams! What in glory's name had kept him from it? He had speed and ball-handling ability, both of which were obvious as he played one of the out positions in this makeshift line-up. And he passed the ball off well. In fact, the more Coach Denton watched, the surer he was that Townsend's passing was nothing short of exceptional.

Assistant Coach Cully Thomas had arranged the ten newcomers into two line-ups. Townsend played on the same "team" as Crickett Sledge, the towering post prospect. At seventeen, Sledge stood an ungainly six-feet-nine inches. His height seemed to be his only asset, but such a reach could be a potent weapon if passes were fed to him skillfully.

And this Craig Townsend kept getting the ball in to the post player. Sledge was taking the short throws at knee height, whirling and stretching, and the defense could do nothing to check the baskets.

To the uninitiated eye, it looked as if Sledge was showing uncanny basket skill. The group of students sitting behind the coach thought so.

"Boy, with that Sledge in there," gloated one of the fans, "we'll murder Warmouth this year. We'll take the conference like Grant took Richmond."

Coach Denton did not share this optimism. The coach, in fact, found the lanky center a bit disappointing. Sledge, he had noted, had practically no defensive ability. And this scoring spree could be discounted considerably. In the first place, Sledge was getting off his shots against another newcomer, Paul Tipton, who stood six inches shorter. In addition, this surprising Townsend was skillfully setting up the center's sweeping hook shots.

Townsend's passes into the post caught Tipton drawn to one side and Sledge already moving away from his guard. Such excellent timing was not accidental as the coach well knew. It was seldom found in high-school players, even the standouts. Yet this boy supposedly had not been good enough to letter in high school.

The two makeshift teams went at it again, with Cully Thomas as referee. One group played barechested; the quintet, including Sledge and Townsend, wore Belmont's blue practice jerseys.

The Blues took the ball out of bounds. Buster

Tolar dribbled past the center line. This boy Tolar showed promise, too; Coach Denton had noted his hustle and sure shooting. He was small, though, for a forward assignment, only about five-ten. And he did not seem rugged enough for defensive work.

Tolar passed off to Townsend. Craig dribbled twice, then feinted a pass in to Sledge. Coach Denton privately admitted that he was prejudiced against fancy dribblers. All they did, he believed, was entertain the spectators. Seldom did even the trickiest ball-bouncing affect the final score.

Townsend pitched back to Tolar, then crossed in front of Buster as if headed for the corner. Craig moved deliberately, allowing Tolar to set for a shot. But instead, Buster speeded up the circling attack, typical of Coach Denton's Belmont teams. In to Sledge, back out to Buster, over to Townsend. The Blue center swung a step ahead of his opposing man, and Craig fed him the ball. Sledge rose up to full height and hooked for the basket.

The attentive coach noted that Townsend moved to a rebound position after his pass. Sledge's basket try hit the hoop and bounded squarely into Craig's waiting hands. The guard started to shoot, then whirled and flipped the ball to Tolar. Townsend stood as a stout screen between shooter and the tangle of players under the basket. Buster calmly sank the basket.

Assistant Coach Thomas blew his whistle.

"Isn't that about enough?" he called out to Denton.

The coach nodded and rose to his feet. "That's enough," he said. "Send 'em all in, all but Townsend."

He handed Craig the ball and gestured to the opposite basket.

"Shoot a few," he said, "while I talk to the old hands."

He called the twelve holdover members of the varsity around him. Six of them were returning lettermen. Three—Frank Hurst, Jamie Brooks, and Perry Stanton—had been starters the previous season.

"Well," the coach demanded, "what do you think of our new talent?"

"I think," Jamie said ruefully, "three of them will make the starting line-up, which means I'll be sitting out this year."

"Not all year," smiled Denton. "The cheerleaders wouldn't stand for it."

Jamie had been selected as the school's best-looking athlete the year before, and he was never allowed to forget it.

"I was a little disappointed in Sledge," said Frank Hurst. "He's awkward, Coach. Won't he foul a lot against good guarding?"

Coach Denton was silent a moment. Frank was the team's veteran shooting ace. The year before, he had set a conference scoring record for first-year players. If Belmont's attack was built around the lanky newcomer this year, then Hurst's point-making would suffer. Was the six-foot-two-inch Frank thinking along those lines? Denton was not sure. It was sometimes hard to distinguish between breeziness in a boy and cockiness. Hurst was certainly one or the other, or perhaps both.

The coach pointed to Craig Townsend, lazily shooting baskets at the other end of the court.

"What about Townsend?"

None of the three veterans answered for a moment. Then Hurst, the captain-elect, said slowly, "He's the big surprise as far as we're concerned, Coach. We didn't think too much of him the first time or two out. But he can sure handle that ball."

"He certainly can," agreed Denton, "and he's tall. Sledge is bigger, sure, and so is Ed Barley. But Townsend has more reach than anybody else."

His musing eyes swept their faces. "How is he to get along with?"

"Oh, easy enough," Jamie Brooks said. "Doesn't have too much to say. Studies pretty hard."

"He has to do that," said Hurst. "He entered on scholastic pro."

Denton nodded. The coach had carefully checked the scholastic standing of every aspirant for his team.

"He has top marks thus far, though," the coach explained. "He'll be off pro by midterm anyhow. And the dean says his instructors would probably clear him now if we asked for it."

Belmont's regulations permitted a student to be taken off the scholastic probation list at any time by the unanimous recommendation of his instructors.

"None of us really knows much about Townsend, Coach," Perry Stanton said. "Nobody paid much attention to him until basketball started. He doesn't mix too much; I can tell you that. I don't believe he's had a date since he enrolled here."

"Does he have a job?"

"No," answered Hurst. "I asked him. He shrugged his shoulders and said he just studied all the time."

"I'll talk to him," Coach Denton said. He hesitated a moment, then added, "Maybe I shouldn't go out on a limb, but this Townsend strikes me as one of the best prospects we've had in a long time."

"Better than Sledge?"

"Sledge is tall," Denton said with a shrug. "A

beanpole always helps a basketball team. The game's made for them. But right now I can't be sure Sledge will help us too much. And I know Townsend can. Okay, boys, let's call it a day. Get a good night's rest. We'll start hitting the boards hard tomorrow. We'll have five days to get ready for Midtown."

"That's right," said Frank, shaking his head. "Time sure slips up."

As the squad trooped off to the dressing room, Denton called to Craig Townsend, "Come into the office, Townsend. I'd like to talk over some things with you."

"Yes, sir," the newcomer said quickly.

✻ ✻ ✻ ✻ ✻

Rangy, narrow-hipped, fairly broad-shouldered Craig Townsend was built like a basketball player. A generation before, mused Coach Denton, the youth would have been a choice physical specimen indeed. In Denton's own playing days, a youth three inches over six feet tall would have been welcome in any cage line-up. But, as every basketball coach moaned, the boys came taller every season. A post man had to tower six-eight or six-nine to attract rave notices. And he had to handle himself well, too.

"Well, Townsend," Denton began, "what do you think of our ball club?"

"Mighty good," Craig replied. "But I don't have to tell you that."

"No," Denton said wryly, "nor the boys either. We aren't bothered with too much modesty, especially Hurst."

Townsend smiled faintly. "He can hit that bucket. That fallaway shot is tough to handle. I don't see how he gets it off without falling on his ear."

"He tries it enough," the coach said dryly. "He ought to be good at it."

Denton frowned up at the rangy youth. "Townsend, this business of your not making the starting line-up at Compton doesn't make sense. You said you were on their squad three seasons ago. I watched them in the state tournament that year, and they didn't get anywhere. Why weren't you playing regularly?"

"Simple," the youth said evenly. "I wasn't good enough."

"Then you've learned a lot of basketball since then," said Denton crisply. "You've been in the service two years, the Air Corps. Surely you didn't pick up that much playing with an air-base team!"

Craig Townsend hesitated, and a grin curved his lips.

"Maybe if I told you who coached that air-base team," he said gently, "you'd find it easier to believe."

"Who was he?"

"Captain Gilbert Wayne."

Denton started. "The ex-pro?"

"Yes, sir. And he coached college basketball at Great Eastern."

"I know," nodded Denton. "Lost his job over—" His voice fell off. Wayne's crack Great Eastern quintet had been involved in a Madison Square Garden scandal. The college had dropped intercollegiate athletics as a result. And Gilbert Wayne had left the coaching ranks.

"I didn't know what ever happened to Wayne," Denton said. "I didn't know him personally, but I've heard some of his lectures. He knew his business, no doubt about it. Here in the Southwest we didn't like his style very much. We like a more wide-open game than his boys played."

"I know," nodded Craig. "He's hipped on ball control."

"Not as rabid as some, though. So he coached you?"

"Yes, sir."

Craig Townsend looked down at the floor a moment, then raised his eyes.

"I think I understand how you feel, Coach," he said slowly. "You're skeptical. You think maybe I'm trying to put something over on you. Or somebody is."

"I didn't say that, Townsend," Denton objected.

"No, not exactly. But you're looking for the catch. There isn't any, I'll promise you that. I could have come to you before the tryouts. I could have said, 'Now, look, Coach, don't pay any attention to my poor high-school record. That was three years ago, and I'm four inches taller and twenty-five pounds heavier. I wasn't worth a darn at Compton, but while I was in the Air Corps they made a good basketball player out of me. You're just lucky I decided to come to Belmont Junior College, for I could have gone almost anywhere. Maybe I could have even gotten a scholarship.'"

Craig chuckled. "If I had come to you with all of that, you would have decided that this Townsend could sure shoot off his mouth. The boys would have had the same notion. They would have been on their toes to show me right away that I wasn't the big shot I thought I was. This way I haven't stepped on anybody's toes, and I've had a fair chance to show what I could do. That's it, Coach, all of it."

"Okay," said the mentor with a nod. "I'm not a man to look a gift horse in the mouth. Gil Wayne taught you to play basketball, and there isn't a better coach of fundamentals in the business. Now why did you come to Belmont? You're paying your own way—at least, so far. Why didn't you go to a senior college? Or to another prep school? Wayne could have helped you get in somewhere in the East."

"He offered to," admitted Craig, "but he advised against it. He's still well known in that part of the country. The papers would have made a little fuss over me as his protégé. I didn't try to enroll in a senior college because I didn't have enough high-school credits. I had to accept scholastic probation to get in here. If I hadn't been a veteran, I couldn't have gotten in even that way."

The puzzled half-frown which the coach's face had worn at the beginning of this conversation was disappearing. All of this made good sense. Craig Townsend's appearance bore out his explanations. He was sure of himself, yet not too cocky. He was accustomed to earning privileges, not currying favors. His army service would have taught him patience, a quality not many junior-college students had.

"And I chose Belmont," Craig went on, "because of your reputation. And because I read that Crickett Sledge planned to come here for more seasoning before trying the college game. I want to be on a championship team. We should have one this year."

Coach Denton frowned. He did not like such optimistic predictions. Already there was too much being printed about Belmont's brilliant cage revival.

"We'll see," he said. "We'll work and hustle and we'll see. We run with some pretty tough outfits. They gang up on the top dogs. The favorite in December is usually an also-ran in February. We'll see. I enjoyed the visit, kid. I'll see you tomorrow."

Chapter Two

Craig Townsend whistled through his shower and as he drove slowly down the main approach to Belmont Junior College. He felt much better after his talk with Coach Denton. All week he had been conscious of the mentor's curious, puzzled study. The boys on the squad had not shown such marked reaction to the newcomer. They had voiced curiosity, yes, particularly when the word got around that three years separated his high-school experience and junior-college enrollment.

His casual explanation, though, quickly silenced their questions. He had enlisted at seventeen and served a two-year hitch. Now he was back in school. He had chosen a junior college because he felt rusty about classwork. He needed a year or so to get ready for college.

Craig's case was not a rare one by any means.

At least a dozen other Belmont students were in the same position. One such veteran, Clarence Ware, had played a standout season at quarterback on the Belmont football team. His teammates had nicknamed him "Pappy" because he was married and the father of a two-year-old daughter.

Ware, however, was a Belmont native. His enrollment at the hilltop school after his discharge was easy to take for granted. The other students had either known him before his enlistment or had heard of him.

This football acquisition had not simply dropped out of the blue as had Craig Townsend, the school's newest athletic surprise. Nor had Ware sat quiet and aloof in his classes, making few acquaintances. His fellow students knew all about him. Craig's teammates, however, could offer little helpful information to those who were curious about him as a new student.

Buster Tolar, for example, could tell his sister Mary only that the new addition to the team looked like a sure starter.

"Where did he come from?" asked Mary. "I had never heard of him until this week."

"He's been here since the term started. Boning up on his courses, I guess. He entered on scholastic pro and he's hustling to get off."

"Well," said Mary with light sarcasm, "I'd like to meet an athlete who studies. You certainly don't."

She was a year older than her freckle-faced brother. Mary had a part-time job in the library, working from 3:00 to 6:00 P.M. She often waited around to walk home with Buster.

"I'm passing my courses," Buster said lightly.

"With my help," his sister pointed out, "and just barely."

Craig Townsend recognized Buster as he drove by. He stopped and backed up.

"Can I take you somewhere, Tolar?" he called out.

"Going south?"

"Any direction you say."

Buster opened the door for his sister.

"Mary, this is Craig Townsend. You've heard me talk about him. My sister, Craig."

Craig acknowledged the introduction with a smile. Then he turned back to Buster.

"I didn't know you had a sister, Tolar. Why don't you tell me these things?"

"It isn't so unusual," Buster said with a shrug. "Quite a few guys have sisters."

"Not like yours," Craig said quickly.

Buster did not challenge that remark. He couldn't, not as appreciative as he was of his sister's attractiveness. Mary had inherited a few freckles of her own, but these were well grouped about her pert nose. She was blue-eyed, brown-haired, and noted for her direct friendliness.

"Thank you, Craig," Mary said. "I didn't expect such a compliment, not from an athlete. But you must be different from what I'm used to. Buster tells me you even bone for good grades."

"Have to. I couldn't enter Belmont except on scholastic pro. If I don't get off before midterm, I can't play basketball this season."

"You can get dispensation right now," scoffed Buster. "The coach checked with your profs. You've nothing lower than a B."

"I think that's fine," Mary said. "Maybe the Army did that for you. Mother worries herself sick about Buster having to go sometime. I tell her it'll be the best thing in the world for him."

"It did me a lot of good," said Craig. "I learned a lot."

"And you saved some money," Buster said enviously. "That's how you rate the car, isn't it? Or did your folks buy it for you?"

"My folks aren't living. I was an orphan when I enlisted."

Mary gestured for Craig to stop before a two-story frame house. Buster voiced thanks for the ride and leaped out. His sister hesitated. She was quite impressed by the lean-faced, soft-speaking Craig Townsend. She thought she would like to know him better. But Mary was thinking more of Buster than of herself when she asked Craig in to meet her mother. This rangy youth was sure to develop into a leader on the basketball squad. He was a year or so older than the other boys, and his army service had given him added maturity. Craig, she was thinking, would be a good influence on Buster.

Her younger brother was no great problem to his family, but Mary shared her mother's concern about his mediocre grades and his apparent lack of purpose and drive.

Craig accepted her invitation after only slight hesitation.

Mrs. Tolar quickly made the visitor feel at home. She was a motherly sort, treating her children's friends as if she had known them a long time. Craig stayed a half hour, leaving only when he realized he was keeping the Tolars from dinner. He firmly refused Mrs. Tolar's invitation to join them.

"I just brought your chicks home, Mrs. Tolar," he said pleasantly. "I didn't come here to board."

"You'll come again, won't you?" she asked.

Craig's eyes went from her to Mary.

"I sure will," he said softly. "At least, I intend to."

Craig still whistled to himself as he drove to the small garage apartment about a mile from the campus where he lived. As he warmed the stew which would be his night meal, he looked around distastefully. He was his own housekeeper, and lately he had been careless about his tasks. There was nothing here, he mused, of the neat, homelike atmosphere which characterized the Tolars' living room.

Craig stretched out on the divan and grinned at his sudden feeling of loneliness. Had the time actually come when he was tired of solitude? How long had it been since he took a girl out for dinner and dancing? Not since he left the service and not one time since he enrolled at Belmont Junior College.

He turned over and flipped on the television set. It was time for Dan Pryor's nightly sports show. Craig closed his eyes and listened indifferently to Pryor's account of a nearby golf tournament.

He sat up as the commentator mentioned the Belmont basketball team. Pryor had watched Belmont's practice the day before.

"Coach Forrest Denton," announced Pryor, "expects to start at least two newcomers in Friday night's opener with Midtown. The Blues boast three proven veterans in Lefty Hurst, Jamie Brooks, and Perry Stanton. Filling out the starting list will probably be Crickett Sledge and Craig Townsend. Sledge, of course, is the highly touted beanpole who set all kinds of scoring records in high school. Not much is known about Townsend, except that Coach Denton plans to pair him with Hurst at forward this year."

Craig scowled. Forward! He didn't want to play forward, especially not in a three-in and two-out offensive pattern. He should be a guard in such a setup. Craig aspired to be a playmaker, not a basket hawk. Gil Wayne had convinced him that such a role promised the brightest future. Craig had no trouble remembering the ex-professional's exact words.

"You gotta work toward the big game, kid. The top leagues in college, the semi-pro circuit, even the pro outfits. Six-three basket hawks come a dime a dozen. But a tall boy who can play out—who can set up plays and get back in a rush on defense—the top teams will want him. Let your buddies make the points in prep school, kid. They don't mean a thing. Sure, be a set-shot boy. And a good one. The zone defense is the answer to a big center, and set shooters are the answer to a zone. But you're a born out-man, kid, and don't let anybody talk you out of it."

So Wayne had coached him, too, for two seasons,

or actually for two full years. Craig Townsend had worked out in the base gym during the off seasons, too. Basketball had been almost his only interest at the post. He had done fairly well in his work as a mechanic and had finally merited a corporal's rating. But, chiefly, in the service he'd learned patience, perseverance, and basketball.

Craig flipped off the television set and filled a plate with stew. Why let a television commentator's statement upset him? Maybe Coach Denton intended to try a two-in and three-out attack. That wouldn't be bad tactics, not with Frank Hurst's jump shooting and Crickett Sledge's rebounding. Certainly with Craig, Jamie, and Perry as out-men, Coach Denton would not have to worry about floor strength.

* * * * *

But the coach said nothing about a change to two-three the next afternoon. This first scrimmage between tentative first and second units found Lefty and Craig as forwards, Crickett as center, Perry and Jamie as guards.

Craig frowned as he took his place near the circle. So the coach insisted on his working in the post with Frank and Crickett! He had played an "in" position some with the air-base team, and he had acquired a good hook shot under Captain Wayne's personal tutelage. Wayne, in fact, had insisted on teaching him every phase of the game, but Craig had no intention of fitting into this pattern. He would play only a minor role in such an attack. Sledge would be in the post as much as the rules permitted and Lefty most of the other times.

The varsity worked the ball in, and Lefty Hurst took a pass from Perry. Frank whirled with his two-handed jump shot. The ball rimmed off, and Eddie Moss recovered for the second-stringers.

As he ran back to his defensive position, Craig realized why Coach Denton preferred three men under the basket instead of two. Hurst could not follow up his favorite fallaway shot. If he missed, the backboard was open as far as one opposing guard was concerned. The defense had an edge on rebounds. In a two-in setup, Crickett Sledge would be left to battle the board singlehanded.

Coach Denton needed a third player with height, without a doubt, but why Craig Townsend? Why sacrifice a smooth backcourt player to cover up for Hurst's weakness? Let Eddie Moss or Mark Kutner move up from the second team to play that other forward spot.

Craig smothered Buster Tolar's effort to shoot,

and the regulars took the ball again. Perry to Jamie—Jamie to Perry—Perry to Craig. Sledge led his guard by half a step; Craig fed the ball in. The lanky center stretched up to shoot. Up, too, went Ed Barley who was six-seven himself. Barley was a holdover who had seen spot service the year before. He was no dead shot with either hand, but he guarded another tall boy fairly well. He knocked off Crickett's hook. Craig scooped up the free ball and pitched to Lefty.

Hurst strained backward, and his push-shot swished through the net.

For ten minutes Coach Denton let his tentative varsity work together. Then the coach whistled a halt to the scrimmage. The score stood 12-3 in favor of the regulars, but neither Denton nor Assistant Cully Thomas was pleased.

"Hurst made nine of the points," Thomas said disgustedly. "And he wasn't hogging the shots, not any more than usual."

Denton stood glumly watching the players as they trotted to the water fountain.

"We were too high on Sledge," he said grimly. "I was afraid of that. And maybe we were oversold on Townsend, too. Neither one of them showed much."

Craig's lean face showed no reaction as he was

23

moved to second-team guard. Actually he had to smother a grin of happiness. For Coach Denton moved Kutner onto the first team, and Craig had both Eddie Moss and Barley to feed.

Barley did not match Crickett Sledge as a scoring threat, but any youth so tall had to be watched carefully.

Buster dribbled down as the Whites got the ball. Craig took a pass and gestured to Moss.

"I'll throw ahead of you," he whispered. "Break slow, and then you'll have to stretch for the ball."

So the painstaking Gilbert Wayne had taught his charges to work the ball. A deliberate break, then a quick lunge to capture a skillful pass, and the forward was free for a quick shot more times than not.

The lean Eddie was six-four and had a long reach. Lefty Hurst took him on defense. Moss swung out of the corner and around the circle. Craig bounced in a well-spotted pass. Eddie barely touched the ball, and it rolled away out of bounds.

Moss snapped his fingers. "Should have had it," he muttered. "I didn't believe you. Didn't drive hard enough."

Craig nodded. An extra bit of effort would have made the play work.

Lefty Hurst sank one of his specialties, and the Whites had the ball again. This time Eddie swung slowly in front of Frank, then broke sharply and quickly. He took Craig's pass on his fingertips and sank his shot.

"Now you got the hang of it," Townsend said with a grin.

Craig watched closely as Perry and Jamie flipped the ball around. What better way to prove his playmaking ability, he thought, than to fire up this so-called second unit? Both Eddie Moss and Buster Tolar nursed first-team ambitions of their own. Both were newcomers also. Well, why not make the most of this chance to show up the overconfident veterans?

Townsend whispered his instructions to Buster. The three of them could deal Coach Denton's so-called varsity a little trouble.

And they did. Moss penetrated the Blue defense for another basket. Then Buster sank a one-hander from the circle. Meanwhile Frank Hurst missed two consecutive tries. Craig's tricky guarding accounted for both failures. He slid off Kutner, supposedly his charge, to block Lefty's usual backward step before his shots.

When Denton halted the scrimmage, the score stood even. The three veterans plus the vaunted Sledge had been played to a deadlock!

The two coaches sent the squad in and retired

to Denton's office to talk over the workout. Neither was pleased.

"Well, I'll go on record about one thing," muttered Cully Thomas. "That Townsend is a natural-born leader and organizer. He's as resourceful a boy as I've seen in a long time."

"You're right about that," agreed Denton. "If he'd drive on the board, he would be the answer to our prayer."

Thomas looked questioningly at his superior. "You don't think Sledge can go in fast company?" he asked.

"I'm afraid he can't," said Denton, "but I don't know anything to do but try him."

"That's how it looks to me," nodded Cully.

Chapter Three

Midtown's Lions had to spot Belmont in both height and experience. Coach Denton was sure he could experiment with several combinations and still record a victory. The chance might not come again; he meant to make the most of it.

He named Craig to start along with Hurst, Sledge, Brooks, and Stanton—the three taller boys in on the attack and the two shorter ones out. Craig suppressed his scowl at the coach's announcement. The bald-headed, easy-mannered mentor, he reflected, was a hard man to convince. Not once in a scrimmage had this grouping worked as well as combinations which had Craig setting up the plays.

It wouldn't work against the Lions either, Craig told himself. Brooks and Stanton couldn't get the ball in to the lanky Sledge, not if the visitors kept a tight defense around the post. And in the early moments of play the Lions showed they meant to do that.

Obviously they knew all about the lanky Sledge's scoring in high school. Midtown's tallest guard stood only six-three. But a second defensive man, of almost equal stature, moved over to help when the Belmont center took the ball. Sledge, usually taking the pass flat-footed, couldn't get his shots away.

The Blues took a 6-3 lead, then a 10-6 advantage. Frank Hurst hit three baskets from the floor, and the two guards made a bucket each. But, during a time out after eight minutes of play, the near-packed Belmont gym buzzed with disappointed whispers. Nothing about the team's showing justified the early visions of a championship team. Neither of the highly-touted newcomers, Townsend and Sledge, had shown much. If they had to depend on Lefty's fallaway shooting, then the Blues were no better off than they were last year.

During the time out, though, Coach Denton sent Mark Kutner onto the floor and pulled off Perry Stanton. That sent Craig to guard, and Townsend hurried to show immediately the difference such a change made.

Jamie worked the ball down, flipped to Craig. He threw in to Sledge without a second's hesitation.

28

His pass led the tall center by a full step. Crickett stretched and almost lost his balance, but he held the pass and received a free try as his Midtown guard bumped him.

Sledge made good from the charity line, repeated the free throw a few seconds later. Craig's crisp passes came in too fast and sure for the second Midtown guard to cover. Sledge got clear for a successful crip, and Belmont led 14-6.

Midtown called for a time out and revamped its defense. Two guards slid over to help check the towering center. Craig promptly shifted his passes to Frank Hurst.

The southpaw goal shot was notoriously a "streak shooter." He would miss several tries in succession, hit a cluster of baskets straight-running, then begin missing again. Craig Townsend quickly learned what the previous year's team had known, to feed Hurst while he was "hot." Lefty sank four field goals in less than two minutes. The visitors tallied three points in that time to make the score 22-9.

Perry Stanton returned to the court for Belmont, along with Buster Tolar, Paul Tipton, Edgar Barley, and Eddie Moss. Craig, pulling on his sweat clothes, grinned in approval as Tolar sank a long set shot. He wanted Buster to make a good showing for Mary's sake as well as the youth's own. Craig looked

29

around at the gallery. Surely she was here tonight, for the first game of the season.

Midtown pulled up slightly against these Belmont substitutes, but not enough to alarm Coach Denton. The half ended with the Blues leading 32-21.

*　*　*　*　*

Craig sat on the bench as the third quarter opened. Coaches Denton and Thomas wanted to see how their veteran guards worked with the basket trio of Hurst, Sledge, and Kutner.

The result was about what Townsend expected. Midtown kept Sledge bottled up while Hurst fired in shots from all over the court. Crickett slapped in two rebounds, with the net result that this combination appeared fairly effective. After six minutes of the period, Belmont had stretched its lead to 46-26. Lefty Hurst, though, had played himself out.

The basket ace had that handicap. He could not hold up his whirlwind pace through an entire game.

Craig led four other teammates, including Ed Barley, onto the court for a few minutes' action. This combination had two scoring weapons—Eddie Moss breaking into the post and Buster shooting from outside the circle. Craig kept both busy. Each scored twice before another time out let the Belmont coaches experiment further.

In this new line-up Moss and Kutner worked as forwards, Sledge as center, and Buster and Craig as guards.

All new faces to the Belmont fans, and the hometown crowd liked what happened. This quintet responded spiritedly to this chance to show what they could do together. Sledge, rested himself now and working against a listless Midtown five, ran wild under the basket. The visitors abandoned their three-on-one to practice their man-for-man, simply letting the tall boy go. He racked up nine points in five minutes while Moss scored four and Buster three.

With seven minutes left, Coach Denton pulled out the new players and sent his veterans back in. An ovation rewarded the newcomers for their scoring outburst. They had pushed the score up to 69-34. If Frank Hurst continued his skillful shooting, the crowd might see a home-court scoring record set.

Lefty shot from all positions, but the Belmont total of 80 fell shy of a new mark. Still an 80-41 decision was impressive. The fans chattered happily as they filed out. If and when Coach Denton settled on a starting line-up, this year's team might go places. And with all the personnel he had, who could blame the coach for shifting the boys around? Who were his five best players? Hurst, of course. Frank had 28 points in this first game of his last year. Sledge, despite his disappointing moments, had tallied 19. Buster Tolar topped the remaining pointmakers with nine.

Most of Belmont's supporters had an understanding of what made a basketball team click. Those who complained that Craig Townsend hadn't done much were in the minority. And his new admirers spoke out quickly in his behalf. True enough, he had scored only one point, on a free try. But just look back at the game's ups and downs. Townsend had been a key figure in every Belmont scoring surge. The rangy newcomer was just what the Blues had needed for a long time—a born playmaker.

    ✿   ✿   ✿   ✿   ✿

The players drove Coaches Denton and Thomas out of the dressing room with their horseplay and raucous talk.

"Let's go into my office," Denton suggested, "where we can hear ourselves think."

Thomas followed him, equally glad to get out of the din.

32

"Well," Denton said, as soon as he had settled in his battered swivel chair, "we took the wraps off our tall boy tonight."

"Yep," grunted Thomas, "we sure did."

The coach's eyes twinkled. "You don't seem very happy about it."

"Are you?" countered Cully.

"No," Denton admitted, "but not too unhappy either."

"I sure am," declared Thomas. "We get just one tall boy with a lot of publicity, and we're picked to win a championship. I'm not even sure that Sledge has helped us."

"Oh, he has helped," said the calm Denton. "Don't get carried away with your pessimism. Think of the boy's nuisance value. The other team stays scared of him. He weakens their defense by just being on the court."

Thomas nodded in agreement. He had to concede that.

"We do have a long way to go," Denton continued. "We need a three-man attack. I can't see to save my soul why Townsend can't be one of those three men."

"He doesn't seem to be much of a shot."

"So far. But Gilbert Wayne worked on that boy by the hour. Craig is a well-trained player if I ever laid eyes on one. There's precious little you and I can teach him; you know that as well as I do."

"I haven't tried," shrugged Cully. "I've figured we had other things to worry about."

"We do," admitted the coach, "but I intend to keep worrying about that, too. I just don't believe that Wayne went to all that trouble without teaching his protégé to shoot. On Wayne's teams every player had to be a dead-eye."

Then he gestured helplessly.

"Well, we can't do everything the first week or two. We've put our show on the road. Maybe we can keep it going a while."

In the next room the enthusiastic players were putting on their clothes. Buster Tolar used the locker next to Craig's.

"Boy, you were on the beam tonight," Buster said enthusiastically. "The way you set up those shots of mine, I couldn't miss them."

"They don't go in unless you shoot 'em right," Craig said lightly.

Buster was fussing with his tie. "Is this on straight?" he asked, frowning at his reflection in the mirror.

"Straight enough. You must have a date tonight."

"Sure. Alice Cameron."

Craig shook his head. He didn't know her.

"A bunch of us are going out to the country club," Tolar explained. "Herbert Petry picks up the check for us out there every time we win a game. Aren't you going?"

"I hadn't heard about it. Is it a team party?"

"Oh, not exactly. There's nothing official about it. Frank goes with Mr. Petry's daughter Celeste. Mr. Petry is a nut about basketball, and he likes to have Lefty bring along the other players. You don't need an invitation; just come on out."

"Reckon not," declined Craig.

"You ought to come," insisted Buster. "You should mix more. I'll take you in if you're bashful."

"Oh, I don't suppose I'm exactly bashful," said Craig with a shrug, "but I wouldn't know any of the girls. I'd just be hanging around."

"You'll never meet anyone if you keep on studying all the time."

"I'm easing up on the studying. I've been off scholastic probation a week now."

"The dean gave you dispensation?"

"Yes."

"That's something," said Buster, somewhat awed. "An athlete with honor-student rating!"

Eddie Moss came up to Buster. "Can't you talk Townsend into going with us?" he asked.

"No luck so far."

"Work on him," urged the forward. "We need transportation."

"What's the matter with your car?"

"Dead battery."

"Golly," groaned Buster. "I was counting on you."

"I've already asked Hurst and Perry. They're full."

"Well," Buster said unhappily, "I guess we're out of luck."

"Work on Townsend," insisted Eddie. "He's our buddy. He made us look good a few times tonight."

But Craig was still reluctant. Finally he asked, "How far is it out to this club?"

"Not far. Five miles, or six," Buster told him.

"I'll run you out there if you think you can find a ride back."

Buster looked at Moss doubtfully. "What do you think?"

"Let's run the risk," Eddie suggested. "Are you going to pick Alice up at home?"

"Yes. And I have to see that Mary gets home, too."

Craig Townsend smiled. "I can see that Mary gets home and take you by Alice's. Just get dressed."

"This Townsend," said Moss with a grin, "is a handy guy to have around."

"Sure he is," agreed Buster. "Maybe we'd better put him on steady."

Mary Tolar accepted the arrangements calmly.

"It's nice of you," she told Craig. "I should have known that Buster would shift the responsibility for me to somebody else."

"He didn't have to work at that. I was standing right there, and I took him up immediately."

Mary accompanied him on the ride out to the club and back.

"You should have gone to the party," Mary said. "Mr. Petry is a big basketball fan. He's a Crownover alumnus and has helped one or two boys from here get scholarships."

"Crownover!"

Craig caught himself. He was on the verge of saying that he had his heart set on a Crownover athletic scholarship. The Comets usually were the best basketball team in the section. More years than not, they rated a place in the NCAA playoffs. Gilbert Wayne had advised him to set his sights on Crownover as the best place for him to play basketball.

"I understand," Mary went on, "that he has promised to do what he can for Frank Hurst."

"Frank's a good shot," Craig said carefully.

Mary studied his lean face.

"Buster says you're the team's real hope," she said. "That you make the plays work. That you're sorta like the quarterback in football."

"Sort of. It's my job to set up the plays."

"And you like that? You're happy for the other players to get all the recognition?"

Craig shook his head. "You're trying to make something out of me that I'm not," he protested. "Maybe the playmaker is an unsung hero to the crowd. I guess he is. But the coaches appreciate him, and the coaches decide who gets the scholarships."

"You're out to get one?"

"Sure. I have to. I'm on my own, Mary."

"You're doing a fine thing, Craig. Coming back to school after two years in the Air Corps . . . not many boys would do that, especially when they have to pull up a poor scholastic record."

"I've almost got that licked, though. I'll be on the honor roll this semester if nothing happens."

"You've studied hard, haven't you?"

"I'll say. I had to get some tutoring, too. Math didn't bother me much; I got a good start in that in the service. But English and history and Latin— I sweated blood."

"Did you have to drive yourself so hard?"

He nodded. "I had to."

He braked the car to a stop before her house.

"Life's been hard for me a lot of the time, Mary," he said thoughtfully. "I flopped in high school. I let the death of my parents throw me into a spin. With my poor grades I couldn't get into any sort of reserve unit. The draft snapped me up. I thought I'd never live through boot camp, and most of the time I didn't care if I didn't. But instead of giving up, I set out to learn to make life a little easier, and to do it for myself.

"I learned some things," he went on. "I learned to plan and to wait, and to get the hard part of a job done first. The breaks go to the guy who's already ahead. There's no point in whining about it. The thing to do is to pull yourself up first and then snatch up the things that come your way."

He grinned. "That's why I've boned this semester. I wanted to get on top of my courses. Now my profs know all about me. They know I made a deal with myself not to have a single date until I had worked off scholastic probation. I told them so. I've proved I could do it, too. Do I have to bone from now on? Of course not. I'm on the downhill grade. The profs are on my side."

"That makes sense," agreed Mary. "How about the basketball team? Can you go about that the same way?"

"Oh, that," he said carelessly. "I'll play my best and take what comes."

He did not attempt to answer her question. She might get the wrong impression. She might consider his attitude a cold-blooded one. She might decide that he thought his role as a playmaker more important than the team's showing. And that was not entirely true, not from Craig's viewpoint. He meant for Belmont to have a winning team. His strategy would help the team in the long run, not hurt it. A championship for Belmont, a scholarship offer from a top university for Craig Townsend. Those two objectives could be achieved at the same time and in the same way.

Chapter Four

Coach Denton chose the same starting line-up for the Clifton game—Hurst and Townsend at forwards, Sledge at center, Stanton and Brooks at guards.

And the Belmont coach did not vary his offensive pattern either. Craig's assignment was to hustle the boards along with his two tall teammates. Perry and Jamie handled the "out" posts, with the former launching the plays.

Perry could work one maneuver well, feeding Frank for left-handed fallaway shots. He and Lefty had played together through Belmont High School; their smooth precision came from years of court association. Jamie was a Belmont native, too, and almost as adept at anticipating Frank's feints.

Neither of the veteran guards, however, clicked as smartly with Crickett Sledge. The lanky center used little deception in his turns and thrusts. He was too big to slip and slide under the basket; he fairly lumbered. And Craig had satisfied himself about one of the center's other characteristics. Crickett could not handle a pass thrown directly at him. He had better control of the pitch that he had to stretch for.

Perry and Jamie tried to feed him; the guards had orders to do that. Their best results came from lob throws that the Clifton guards couldn't reach. Crickett handled these pitches almost to perfection. Rising up on his tiptoes, or even leaping slightly if he had to, Sledge took the ball high in the air and either shot or passed off to Frank. The lanky youngster held the ball only for fleeting seconds, often merely slapping his pass or shot instead of getting a tight grip on the leather.

Craig Townsend had little part in this pattern of attack. There was an assignment for him, of course. Coach Denton wanted him to drive in on the boards behind the basket tries by Sledge and Hurst. Lefty's shots, in particular, were of the all-or-nothing variety. Either they plopped into the basket, or Belmont lost control of the ball.

But the role Denton chose for Craig was exactly what Gilbert Wayne had advised him against. A six-three youth could help a junior college outfit with his rebound play, but what university scout would realize his potential? Any fairly tall boy could perform that chore. A six-three boy who did no more would be the forgotten player in any line-up.

Craig went through the motions of his position. He took what rebounds he could get and fed them back to Perry or Jamie. Then the two floor men repeated their maneuvers all over again, gesturing the Blues into a weave, finally throwing in to either Sledge or Hurst.

Coach Denton left his starting line-up unchanged for almost ten minutes. Belmont piled up a lead, to the delight of the packed gallery. The Blues had an 18-12 advantage when substitutes came into the game for both teams. But neither of the Belmont coaches was pleased, and the Blue regulars were disgruntled with themselves.

"I don't know what's wrong with us," Frank muttered to Coach Denton. "We don't have any touch."

"You're not mixing up your plays, for one thing," the mentor pointed out. "You're running and shooting, shooting and running. No variation of speed, no change of tactics."

Craig's eyes gleamed. He was glad that Coach Denton realized Belmont's playmaking weakness. Maybe, if and when Craig got another chance at guard, the coach would quit doubting the difference between one playmaker and another.

The Blues' second-stringers had all sorts of trouble with the visitors. Neither Kutner nor Moss could get off clear shots, and big Edgar Barley was nearly useless on offense. The veteran substitute center strengthened the squad to some extent; he could fill in for Sledge occasionally and hold up his end of the defensive burden. But this Belmont second team had to depend chiefly on its two guards for its baskets.

Craig, speculating about the personnel he would like to have helping him in future games, watched Buster Tolar thoughtfully. Buster's accuracy on long shots was uncanny. He hit two buckets from outside the circle and drew out the Clifton defense. Mary's kid brother was slight and none too speedy. But, mused Craig, he could help a team with his long shots, especially if paired with an experienced guard who could cover up for his defensive weakness.

Maybe, reflected Craig, Belmont's best line-up would prove to be himself, Hurst, Sledge, Buster, and either Eddie Moss or Mark Kutner. Coach Denton would be a hard man to convince of that, though. Bench two starting guards from last year's club? What mentor wouldn't be dubious about taking such a step?

But, Craig decided, that line-up would utilize all of this squad's offensive talent. It would throw a big load on him. He would have to play a prodigious backcourt game. He'd have to move like a dervish to set up every play and still keep the Blue attack varied.

Clifton pulled up to within one point of Belmont, 26-25, with four minutes left in the first half. Coach Denton signaled for his team to take time out. Buster, Barley, Kutner, and Paul Tipton came to the bench. Craig, Hurst, Sledge, and Jamie took the floor.

Craig took a deep breath. This was very near to the combination he wanted established as the starting line-up. The Blues were fresh after their rest. Clifton's starters were still in the game except for their center. Now, thought Craig, was the time to prove what the Blues could do with the right playmaker.

His teammates were eager, too. They had a poor earlier showing to make up for. And Craig sensed that Lefty Hurst ached to bring his individual record up to par. The Blue captain sorely needed a flurry of baskets to bring up his average. A junior collegian hoping for a Crownover scholarship could not afford off nights.

So Craig planned the next four dizzy minutes around Frank Hurst. They could go at top speed the rest of this half. The rangy ball-handler set the pace himself. His passes went straight and hard to Frank, to Sledge, off to Eddie Moss.

His determination infected the other regulars. Frank staged one of his typical single-handed sprees. The southpaw basket ace drew the Clifton defense to him; the grim Belmont playmaker shifted to Moss and Sledge as targets for his passes.

Swish—swish—swish! The blue-jerseyed youths dropped in the goals with monotonous regularity. The delighted crowd was caught up in the frenzy of this breathless surge. Clifton's defense fell apart. Two time outs failed to "cool off" the Belmont basket hawks. When the half finally ended, the score stood 43-27.

Craig grinned as he followed his teammates into the dressing room. Could Coach Denton doubt any longer that his Blue team clicked better with Craig Townsend at guard? Hadn't the coach seen in those last four minutes who was obviously his best play-maker?

And Coach Denton was convinced. He was thinking as he looked over his squad that a coach seldom gained success by requiring his players to fit exactly into any pattern he prescribed. Boys simply didn't fit that smoothly. Human equations always bobbed up to change formulas. Some such human equations were puzzles, difficult—or well nigh impossible—to solve.

This Craig Townsend, for instance. Why was he a whirling, hard-driving, confident leader at one position but not at another? Welcome such new leadership for his team? Of course Forrest Denton did. Any coach would. But why couldn't Townsend spark and guide the team from forward as easily as from a backcourt position?

Denton sighed. He couldn't answer that question. But he was now ready to accept what seemed inevitable. Belmont's squad had a new leader. Craig Townsend had replaced Frank Hurst. These boys didn't yet realize what had happened, but the coach no longer doubted it.

He signaled for quiet.

"We're beginning to hit our stride," he said calmly. "We could keep on against Clifton and probably set some new scoring records. But the only record important to us is an unbeaten record in conference play. So let's forget about tonight and get ready for the games ahead, the tougher games."

"Sure, Coach," spoke up Frank. "That's the way we want it."

Denton's lips twitched. Lefty still considered himself the squad's spokesman. Well, the coach would go along with that. But what he had to say was meant more for Craig Townsend than for Frank. He would look to Townsend rather than to Hurst for the execution of his strategy.

"We need to improve our scoring under the basket. Sledge and Frank are doing fine. But we're playing two in and three out, not the other way around. We need to work that third man in for crips and rebounds. Mark and Eddie are coming along all right. We can't have the other side double-teaming either Crickett or Frank. Clifton is trying it, but they're not making it work. Let's start now building up a three-man punch."

"We can work Moss clear, Coach," Craig Townsend said. "It's just a matter of getting used to it."

Denton frowned. He had said "Mark or Eddie." He had not yet decided that Moss held an edge over Kutner. But in this short time the coach had developed a wholesome respect for Craig's court judgment. Maybe Moss had showed more ability, and the coaches had been too busy with other problems to realize it.

"We'll work with both of them," said the coach,

"and see what happens. We'll start off with Eddie."

The squad was back on the court when Denton realized that he had not announced who would open the second half at the guard positions. The coach gestured to Perry Stanton.

"We'll try Jamie and Craig back," the mentor said gently, "but you'll be in there, don't worry about that."

"Sure," Perry agreed with an effort at lightness.

The coach shook his head as he walked to the bench. The saddest duty of his profession was this act of deciding to sideline one youth in favor of another.

Craig and Eddie Moss swapped talk before the jump.

"Well," Eddie said softly, "I'm getting a chance."

"You'll make it," Craig said encouragingly. "Remember to drive hard. Don't let up because I don't seem to see you. I never tip off the pass by watching the man. And I'll lead you every time. Just go hard and watch for the ball."

"I'll drive," Moss promised, "and I won't look back."

The referee signaled for play to open. Sledge tapped the ball backward, and Craig leaped up to take it. He flipped off to Jamie, then took the ball back as the Blue hurried across the line. He feinted to Sledge, passed off to Jamie. Brooks dribbled twice, threw to Frank. Hurst feinted his fallaway shot and threw to Craig.

Townsend passed quickly. Eddie Moss had broken out of the corner under the basket. Eddie took the bouncing throw and angled his shot off the board. It swished through.

Coach Denton's eyes gleamed. This was the kind of attack he wanted to develop. Crickett Sledge could be smothered by a defense which could match his height, and Lefty Hurst's shooting was not consistent. But quick drives into the basket would pay off regularly.

Thirty seconds later Eddie broke from the opposite side of the court and repeated his crip shot. Then, as Clifton abandoned its sliding zone defense for a man-to-man, Sledge started working into the open. Jamie fed lob passes to the tall center; Craig bounced hard ones right into the pivot meleé.

After seven minutes of play Coach Denton decided to use both Mark and Eddie and let Hurst rest. The Blue captain glowered as he pulled on his sweat clothes. Frank realized the soundness of the coach's plan, but he couldn't help being a bit disgruntled. He had meant to set an individual scoring record for the conference this season, as well as repeating on the all-conference team. This business of developing new pointmakers was fine, but Frank did not want it carried too far.

Craig, in turn, was pleased to have Hurst on the bench temporarily. No court man could claim a share in Lefty's baskets. Hurst's shots required only his own skill, not timely, expert feeding from a field general.

The lean guard drove his teammates harder. He had them nearly spent with exhaustion after ten minutes of action. But he had a score of 68-34 to gloat over when Coach Denton put in an entirely new line-up.

Frank worked with this new combination and got off enough shots to satisfy him. Hurst, in fact, sank the field goal which broke Belmont's previous scoring record for a single game. With ten seconds left and the fans pleading for a new mark, the left-handed youth got two free throws. He sank both to make the final score 81-43. And by these conversions he won high-point honors again, nosing Crickett out 20 to 19.

❄   ❄   ❄   ❄   ❄

Craig waited impatiently for Buster to finish romping in the showers. Finally the boy came to his locker, still dripping wet.

"Is Mary here?" Craig asked quickly.

"Sure," answered her brother. "She won't miss a home game this year. And she'll make as many of the trips as she can."

"Does she have a date?"

"I don't think so," Buster said uncertainly. At noon his sister had mentioned something about meeting Ralph Paxton in the library after the game. But Buster was eager to encourage Craig. Mary could get out of that library commitment somehow.

"I'm exempt in all my courses," Craig said. "No mid-term examinations to bother about. I'm off scholastic pro and on the honor roll without hitting another lick. And, as the cowboys say, I'm ready to cut loose a wolf."

"I don't blame you. And on top of that, you made the team tonight for sure."

"Maybe so," Craig said with a smile. He certainly should have, he thought to himself.

"Find Mary," urged Buster. "Talk her into going out with you. Come with Eddie and me to the club. Mary needs to get out more, and Lord knows you do."

"I'll try it," said Craig.

He had very little difficulty. Mary, in fact, had been wondering if Craig would ever ask her for a date, now that he had satisfied his pledge to himself.

Chapter Five

Herbert Petry's parties were always informal. Almost anyone connected in any way with the Belmont basketball team was welcome to attend, and many did. Petry had starred in the sport both for the Blue and for Crownover University. A big, bluff man, he greeted Craig warmly.

"I've been wondering about you," said the wealthy Belmont alumnus. "I asked the boys what kept you away. What's this I hear about your jumping off scholastic pro and onto the honor roll?"

Craig explained.

"You have a fine attitude, young man," Petry commended him, "a very fine attitude. And you play a good game of basketball. You don't score, but I'm not fooled by that. I can appreciate a good playmaker even if the newsboys can't."

Craig hesitated for a moment and then said quietly, "I'm not worried about the sports writers. I can't eat publicity. But I do hope some university scouts pay some attention to me."

Craig waited hopefully and was not disappointed.

"They will, son," Petry promised. "Don't you worry about that. Good playmakers are harder to find in prep school circles than goal hawks. The scouts hear all about the high-point men without half trying. The guards and feeders are what they comb the bushes for."

Craig Townsend hid his smile. Petry's remark reminded him of Captain Gilbert Wayne's advice.

Mr. Petry and Craig were talking several steps away from the dance floor. Most of the other players were taking advantage of the combo's lively music. Mary had been claimed as a partner by Paul Tipton, who had not brought a date.

"Tell me something about yourself," invited the alumnus.

Craig made a good show of reluctance. Actually he had looked forward to meeting Mr. Petry for two weeks—ever since he learned that the enthusiastic Blue supporter was also a prominent Crown-over alumnus. Craig recited the facts briefly. That way, he had learned, he made the best impression. What he had to tell was strengthened by his own understatement. It was an account of an unusual ambition and determination, as his listener quickly realized.

"Say, you did come here meaning business," said Petry. "You took some bad breaks and turned them to your own advantage. Like learning your basketball in the Air Corps."

"And growing, too," said Craig with a modest smile. "I was sort of a runt when they took me in."

"Now, I suppose, you'll be thinking about a university next?"

"Yes, sir. I'm carrying some extra hours of work. By going to summer school, I'll be able to enter a university next fall as a sophomore." Craig waited a moment, then added, "If, that is, I can figure out some way to support myself."

"You're completely on your own?"

"Yes, sir."

"You'll end up a better man for it. Most youngsters have things too easy."

"That hasn't been true with me for three years."

"And look at you," Petry said approvingly. "You're more mature than the average junior-college boy. You're surer of what you want and how you'll get it. I haven't seen you dancing. Don't you like to dance?"

"Oh, yes, sir," Craig said quickly. "I learned to

dance in the Air Corps, too. I took dancing lessons."

"You did!"

"Yes, sir. I figured it would help my basketball. And I believe it has."

"I'm sure of it," Petry said. "Well, I used to cut quite a caper myself. Now I just stand around and watch youth have its fling. Don't let me keep you, son. You can gab with old codgers like me when there aren't so many pretty girls around."

"I'm enjoying it, Mr. Petry," Craig insisted. "Besides, my date seems to be enjoying herself with her partner."

"Then grab another girl. Have you danced with Celeste yet?"

"No, sir."

Craig had, in fact, received only a casual introduction to Celeste Petry.

"Don't be bashful. Celeste isn't really dangerous; she just looks it. Wait here and I'll get her for you. I'll do the tagging if you're too shy."

Craig looked after the broad man as he broke in on his daughter and Frank Hurst. Well, gloated the youth, he had apparently made a good impression on Mr. Petry. He needed such a contact with Crownover's athletic staff. The more Craig thought about it, the surer he was that Crownover offered him the best opportunity of any university. Gilbert

Wayne had advised his protégé to play semi-pro basketball rather than professional. Especially had Wayne urged that course after learning that Craig intended to get an engineering degree. The Army coach had said that with such a degree and a basketball reputation to boot, Craig would be a cinch for a good job with an oil company. That would be a good deal from any angle. The pro game offered no kind of security.

In a moment Mr. Petry came back leading his daughter.

"Honey, this is Craig Townsend. He's as shy about asking a girl to dance as he is about taking a shot at the basket."

"He gets results on the court," Celeste said. "I just hope he does as well dancing."

"I give both the old college try," Craig declared. "Thanks, Mr. Petry. You're the best pal I've found yet."

A minute later Celeste Petry brushed a wisp of hair back from her forehead and looked up at him.

"I'm sorry I had any doubts about your dancing," she said. "Somebody has given you some pointers."

"One or two," Craig admitted.

"Is it true what I hear?" Celeste asked. "That you didn't have a date until you worked off probation?"

"Yes."

"And that you're on the honor roll now?"

"Yep," Craig said lightly. "Exempt in every course. Next week I play and catch up on my sleep while the peasants study."

"I'll be doing my share of it," Celeste said distastefully. "I've just got to pass everything. Dad says I don't get a new car unless I do. And I'm afraid he means it this time."

"Hasn't he before?"

"Not every time," Celeste smiled. "I can usually handle him."

"I'll bet you can. Him or any other man."

Her eyes mocked him. "Are you worried about yourself?"

"No," Craig said promptly.

The music stopped, but Celeste made no motion to walk away from him.

"And why not?" she asked.

"I wouldn't interest you," Craig said calmly. "I'm no rich man's son, no social butterfly. I work hard at basketball and studying. I don't have loose change to throw around. A pretty girl like you can't waste her time on me."

"I trust," Celeste said slowly, "you are flattering me."

"Of course. What else?"

58

"I'm not sure what else," Celeste said. "You, Craig Townsend, are not a typical Belmont product. I have a sneaking suspicion you are making fun of me."

"No, ma'am," denied Craig. "I wouldn't dream of that."

Just then Frank Hurst came up to claim Celeste as a partner. Craig walked off with a smile lurking around the corners of his mouth. He had played all his cards right this night, he thought. He had proved himself the key man in Belmont's record attack. He had made a good impression on a prominent Crownover alumnus. And he could be sure also that he had aroused the interest of Celeste Petry.

He wondered if the latter might not turn out to be something of a major development. Quite obviously her doting father gave her everything she wished. Maybe the surest way to get Mr. Petry's recommendation to Crownover's coaching staff was through his daughter.

He noticed that Celeste's eyes had followed him. Craig's lips twitched. She was not only spoiled but blessed with exceptionally good looks. She was accustomed to getting quick admiration from her fellow students at Belmont Junior College. Probably every male student there envied Frank Hurst, her steady boy friend. But Craig had treated her as if these things did not matter to him. He hadn't bothered to put on any pretense for her benefit. He had invited her interest but had not sought her approval.

And she had said he wasn't a typical Belmont product! His grin broadened. He certainly had not let her think he was overwhelmed by her. He was sure that the young man who did that made a grave mistake. Celeste impressed him as the type of girl who wanted to keep a number of suitors dangling and jumping through a hoop at her command.

Craig found a chair and gave more attention to his surroundings. What would the boys of his old detail think if they could see him lolling at ease in such an expensive club? Quite a step up for a grease monkey, he mused, a yardbird! Well, he would use the same two springboards for other climbs upward. Basketball stardom, academic standards—he could use them to gain social acceptance anywhere. A scholarship would see him through his university years if he managed his approaches wisely. During the summer months he could play in the Eastern recreation resort leagues.

By the time he had a degree, he would be on friendly terms with many men as influential as Herbert Petry. He would have been a welcome guest in country clubs more exclusive than this. His basketball prowess and his college degree would open almost any door for him. Craig's thoughts went back to Captain Gilbert Wayne. "Look at me," Wayne had argued. "Two college degrees, both snaps to get. An athletic reputation. So what am I in the Army? A captain on his way to being a major. Did I have to earn these bars in combat? Not me. I'm a basketball headliner and a college graduate. I'm assigned to physical training. But I paid the price, youngster. I learned the hard way. I was good at my trade. Say I took the glory road all the way if you want to. That's what some of these non-coms think anyhow. The gold-brick route, they call it. I don't deny it. I finally got a little bit smart. The gold in this gold brick was 21-carat metal. If you're going to follow in Wayne's shoes, you have to play basketball like Wayne. When you're the playmaker Wayne was and the boys in the trade know it, you won't miss meals. But it's a long way up that road, kid. You don't cover the distance loafing."

Craig Townsend sighed. His Air Corps tutor had not exaggerated the effort and the patience it took. And, golly, how carefully he had to move. Was well-meaning Coach Denton convinced yet that Townsend belonged in the backcourt, not working the boards? And would Craig really build up a wide reputation as the key man in this strong Belmont quintet?

The fans and the sports writers hadn't realized his real value yet, not by a long shot. As far as they were concerned, Frank Hurst was still the standout performer. In their estimation, Crickett Sledge came next. Well, nothing could be done about that. Somebody had to put the ball in the basket if Belmont was to win.

But, decided playmaker Townsend, there was no real reason why Hurst had to hog the scoring. Maybe there was a surefire way to distract some of the attention from the southpaw veteran. Eddie Moss had potential as a scorer himself. Maybe if Eddie took high-point honors a time or two, Lefty Hurst's prestige would decline.

Craig pushed to his feet. That kind of planning could be left until later. He had already done much that he had set out to do. He could see that he had a lot more still to do. But tonight he had better concentrate on cinching social acceptance. He wanted to be sure of his welcome at such parties in the future.

There were girls here he hadn't danced with. And he had not danced with either Mary or Celeste Petry often enough.

The language which Craig Townsend used when he talked to these coeds was quite different from that of his teammates. His years in the service had taught him formal politeness and tricks of flattery. He was well aware of the good impression he made, too.

"I would say," Mary said on their way home, "that you were the hit of the party. You surprised me, I'll tell you frankly. I thought you'd be bored stiff, but you ate it up."

"Of course," he admitted. "Look, I didn't pass up all the fun of campus life because I wanted to. I get a kick out of acting like a kid."

"You keep talking like you're so much older than everybody else. You're just a year older than I am."

"It's the way I've felt. Tonight I haven't felt that way. Look, I haven't mixed with kids my own age since I was a junior in high school."

"But you *can* mix," Mary pointed out. "You just haven't wanted to go to the trouble."

"That wasn't it," Craig said. "Not exactly, anyhow. I had to prove something first."

"That you could."

"I suppose that's it."

"Well, you can," she declared. "So quit being so self-conscious. Even Celeste Petry went for you." Mary's lips tightened. "Of course you're a new boy," she added lightly. "That always challenges Celeste. She wants to be sure you know how rich her father is."

"I don't know," Craig said calmly. "How rich is he?"

"He's loaded. And does he rate with Crownover! Their coaches spend weekends with him and things like that."

"The basketball coach, too?"

"Certainly. Buster has met him."

"Bart Millican?"

"Yes."

"Bart Millican hasn't built his teams by conning rich alumni," Craig said slowly. "He's one of the best."

"He's supposed to be," agreed the sports-wise girl. "But Herbert Petry calls the shots as far as Belmont Junior College is concerned. Just write down in your little book that Frank Hurst will get a full scholarship to Crownover."

"He might," Craig said slowly. "Right now I guess it looks like it. But it's a long time until March. Lefty might not average 26 points a game from now on."

"What's to stop him? He did last year with a weaker team than this."

"Last year he was a one-man show," the guard

said. "Some of the other boys can hit that basket, too. Crickett's a threat any second. Eddie Moss will improve."

Mary tossed her brown head. "Just the same," she said, "I'll bet you Frank Hurst gets a Crownover scholarship."

Craig shook his head. He didn't care to bet until he knew more about the odds. It was entirely possible that Herbert Petry would be the one to decide which Blue graduate merited a scholarship at his alma mater.

Chapter Six

Coach Denton agreed with the sports writers that Winston offered the first real test for his Blue hopefuls. The Wildcats had finished third in the conference the previous season. Belmont had divided the two-game series with them, winning at home and losing a one-point decision in the Winston gym.

"We play the first game here," the coach told his cagers, "and that's a help. But three nights later we return the visit. Last year that turned out to be a different story. We can't let history be repeated. If we've lost a conference game by the time we get to Warmouth and Hampton, we might as well forget about the championship."

For five full days his squad's workouts had been hampered by mid-term examinations. All the players had missed one or more practices except Craig Townsend. Lefty Hurst, threatened with ineligibility unless he passed four examinations, had not been out a single time.

"Exams set us back every year," the mentor continued after a pause. "We have four days to make up for the time we've lost. Let's hit it, every man. Ease up on your social life until we're past this series."

A murmur of agreement came from the players.

"We're ready, Coach," promised Hurst with a grin. "Me especially. I sure felt good when I saw that English grade."

"Oh, you made it with room to spare, Frank," the coach said dryly. "You passed by three whole points. I don't know what we were so worried about."

"Any landing you can walk away from," answered the captain, "is a good landing. Isn't that what they taught you in the Air Corps, Townsend?"

"No," Craig said truthfully. "They taught us to check a motor the night before. Then there wasn't any question about the ship's making it."

"You're a big help," Lefty grunted.

"All right, gentlemen, let's stop the bull session," Denton said crisply. "Let's have ten minutes of ball-handling, then some scrimmage. Frank, you take Moss, Sledge, Townsend, and Tolar. Coach Thomas will line up a combination from the other boys. When we start, let's go at it hard."

"Yes, *sir*," Lefty said airily. "We'll show up Cully's mullets."

Hurst, thought Craig, seldom let an opportunity pass to ridicule the substitutes. His cockiness of boyhood had not worn off at all. What Frank needed, Craig mused, was basic training experience. He had come out of that a little less eager to throw his weight around.

Craig and Buster paired off for ball-handling drill.

"Did you hear what the man said?" asked Buster. "I'm working with you on the first string."

"That's good," Craig answered. "Keep hustling and you'll get along."

"You think this means anything, Craig?"

Mary's brother was so dead serious that Craig hesitated about answering. He wanted to encourage Buster but not to build up any false hopes.

"Coach might be thinking about a tight zone, Buster," he said finally. "From outside you can hit better than Brooks or Stanton or me either."

"How do we know how you can hit?" grunted Buster. "When do you shoot?"

"When I have to," Craig said casually. "You ought to work the ball in when you can."

Coach Denton prescribed game conditions for this scrimmage, with Cully Thomas as referee.

Craig wondered at the coach's choice of a first-string line-up. Buster working at guard? What was so wrong about that, now that Craig thought about it? The slight youth could sink those set two-handers. And couldn't Belmont use a four-player offensive weave around one playmaker?

Anyhow, Tolar's insertion into the first-string line-up gave Craig another shooter to feed. It just could be, he mused, that Lefty Hurst's personal point-making would become less and less vital to Belmont's cage success.

The defense unit had Kutner, Barley, Stanton, Brooks, and Paul Tipton. Two of last year's starters demoted to the second string . . . that showed the coach's willingness to experiment.

Craig flipped to Buster, took a return pass. He faked a drive and a pass to Frank, then threw to Moss coming out of the weave. Craig and Eddie passed between Tolar and the basket. Moss fed Tolar the ball and Craig yelled "shoot." Buster took dead aim, and the ball swished through.

The substitutes had no offensive gun. Sledge batted away a pass intended for Stanton. Tolar scooped up the free ball and broke down-court. He was fast with his dribble; Perry had to scramble desperately to stop a crip. Buster threw to Craig. Crickett lumbered into the circle and took the ball. The lanky center's hook caught Barley unprepared.

Ten seconds later Sledge took a floor pass and handed off to Eddie. The new forward sank an easy crip.

Cully Thomas called a short breathing spell and walked over to Denton.

"We don't have a one-man attack this season," said Cully. "Not against our subs."

"That's the truth," Denton agreed. He was well pleased with his regulars. This second-team unit was not weak defensively. The coach would be willing to trust this line-up to hold a lead against almost anybody.

Cully blew his whistle, and the scrimmage began again. The coaches let the play go on for ten minutes. In that time the new first string posted a 22-5 advantage.

Of those 22 points, Frank Hurst netted exactly four. Only one time did he get off his favorite fallaway shot for a field goal.

When the boys came to the side lines, Coach Denton passed out some words of praise. Buster Tolar especially glowed at the mentor's compliments.

"Keep hustling, Buster," said Denton, "and we'll use you some this year. We'll have to."

Craig hummed to himself as he stripped off his sweat-soaked uniform. This, to his way of thinking, had been their most satisfactory scrimmage of the season.

"Townsend?"

Craig looked up. Lefty stood just behind him. "Yep?"

"You handled that ball today," said the captain. "I've been thinking about it. You're the best play-maker we ever had here."

"I'm getting used to the boys," Craig answered with a grin. "I think we're showing better teamwork every time out."

"We're doing one thing," Frank said slowly. "You're taking the pressure off of me. I just stood around out there today."

"We know what you can do," Craig said lightly. "If we can develop these other boys to where they can carry some of the load, you'll do better. We won't make baskets like this against Winston."

"No," agreed Frank. "That's the point I'm getting around to. It looks like you're on the first string to stay. And you haven't worked much with me."

"No," admitted Craig. "And you're right. I just thought we ought to learn the other first." He paused, and then said carefully, "I don't care too much for these one-man attacks, Hurst. I think we can win a championship if we don't fall into the rut.

I don't mind telling you that we won't make that mistake with me in there."

"You're getting me wrong, Townsend," Frank said quickly. "I like the way you're setting up plays. Maybe Perry did depend on me too much. I just want to get the feel of your passing. I always sensed when Perry would feed me the ball. I want to get that sure of you."

"Okay," Craig promised lightly. "We'll work on it."

Craig finished dressing. Eddie and Buster had asked for rides; he waited for them. Coach Denton came over to talk with Moss.

"You're picking up, kid," said the coach. "You're picking up right along. But you're losing the ball too often going up on the boards. You got to follow through with that shot even if you've been fouled or somebody has batted at the ball."

"I know," sighed Eddie. "I don't have the best hands in the world. My high school coach used to tell me that."

"You can stand some improvement," agreed Denton, "but don't start pressing."

"Wouldn't some shooting practice at night help?" Moss asked eagerly. "Could I check out a ball and come back after supper?"

"And just shoot?"

"Yes, sir. Work on holding the ball tighter."

"The gym will be open, and you can have a ball," said Denton with a smile. "Help yourself."

Eddie told Buster and Craig that he intended to return after supper for more practice.

"Why don't you come, too?" Moss asked Tolar. "You're on the borderline just like me. Some extra practice wouldn't hurt you."

"I'm sure willing. I'll meet you here at eight o'clock."

"It's a deal," agreed Eddie.

After letting Moss out, Craig drove Buster home.

"Come in for supper," the freckle-faced boy invited as he started to get out of the car. "Mother has been fussing because I haven't brought you."

Craig refused at first but finally gave in.

"You can cancel the invitation, Mrs. Tolar," he told Buster's mother, "and there won't be any hurt feelings. This son of yours ought to be more careful about inviting people to meals."

"He was careful," Mrs. Tolar said promptly, "and you were foolish to argue with him. Of course it will upset Mary when she gets home."

"Why?" Craig asked innocently.

"Why? Well, why not? From what I hear, you're a cool cat, or whatever the phrase is. These kids change their jargon so often I'm never quite sure what I'm repeating."

"You do pretty well," said Buster with a grin. "There are cats and squares and offbeats. Also mullets. Townsend is a cat."

"I don't understand it either," Craig told Mrs. Tolar. "I finally learned the Air-Corps lingo. That took me two years."

"And you come back to the civilian world and don't understand a thing you hear."

"I figure out most of it," Craig answered. "What I want to, anyway. I understood Buster when he invited me to eat."

Mary's eyes lit up when she came in and saw Craig.

"How did you manage it?" she asked Buster. "I've started to ask him several times. But my mother taught me not to be a designing hussy."

"She tried to," teased Mrs. Tolar. "I wouldn't say she succeeded."

"Females," Buster told Craig, shaking his head. "They wrangle all the time."

Craig chuckled. He couldn't think of anything more pleasant than this closely-knit family. Their enjoyment of each other spread to everyone around them. Did they realize how fortunate they were? He doubted if they did. Only someone like himself, who had known no sort of home since his early teens, realized what they had.

Mrs. Tolar's meal was what he might have expected—well prepared, well balanced. Mary ate almost as enthusiastically as Buster and his guest.

"I don't see how she does it," Mrs. Tolar sighed, "without getting fat. I guess it's because she's always on the go."

"I have to be," said Mary. "Between school and my job and coaxing a brother to study, I must keep going."

"No tutoring tonight," announced Buster. "I'm going back to the gym and work with Eddie Moss."

"Good thing," Mary said. "I have to go to the library myself."

"I'll drive you," Craig offered quickly.

"What's this extra practice for?" Mary asked her brother.

"Eddie and I are crowding the regulars," explained Buster. "We want to crowd them harder."

"Are they really, Craig?"

"The coaches think so," Craig told her. "Both Eddie and Buster worked first string today."

Her blue eyes studied him thoughtfully. "Are you going to help them?" she asked finally.

"Me? What could I teach them?"

"I imagine," Mary said gently, "you could help

them a great deal. You seem to have figured out this basketball business from A to Z. And most everything else about junior college, too."

He looked at her intently. What had inspired such a comment?

As the three young people started to leave, Mrs. Tolar invited Craig to come back often. And he meant his promise to drop in again.

"Why don't you come on to the gym with me, Craig?" asked Buster as they drove off.

"I might at that," agreed Craig. "Especially if Mary will let me take her home when she's through at the library."

"That's a deal," promised the girl. "I'll come by the gym."

Eddie Moss was already waiting at the gym. The slim forward grinned when he saw Craig in his sweat suit.

"I was hoping you'd help us. I would have asked you myself, but I didn't have the nerve. What do you think I need to work on most?"

"Your driving," Craig said without hesitation. Now that he was sure his help would not be resented, he felt no reluctance to give it. "You have to use your body. Screen the ball with it. Here, guard me coming in and I'll show you."

Captain Gilbert Wayne had trained his young

protégé in board drives just as well as in backcourt play. From Wayne, Craig Townsend had learned the skill which usually came only from long experience. He had been taught to hook his shots with either hand, to roll them off the backboard when the net was blocked.

The clever player went in to the basket with the ball screened by a shoulder or an elbow.

"Your trouble," he told Eddie, "is that you're depending on your reach alone. "You're six-four, aren't you?"

"That's right," Eddie told him.

"That was tall in junior high school. It isn't here. If you go up with your reach, the defense is on top of you. Guys like Ed Barley and Crickett Sledge can just smother you from on high. Feint away from them just before you shoot. Try to pull them in to you or on top of you. Buster, you watch for fouls."

Craig proved his point time after time. Lunging in and upward, he managed always to keep a shoulder or an elbow between the ball and Eddie's thrusts.

"Lord, Townsend," Eddie panted after a few minutes, "you ought to be in the keyhole yourself. You're so fast with that ball that I can't keep up with you."

"I'm not juggling the ball around so much," Craig explained. "I'm doing most of the faking with my body and shoulders. That's how Hurst gets off so many of his shots, except that he's hipped on just one maneuver. If he'd use more fakes, he'd be even harder to guard."

"I've guarded him," said Moss, "and you're harder to cover than he is."

"Better shot, too," Buster put in. "If we didn't need you back, you could move right in as a forward."

"I don't want to, though," Craig said sharply. "We'll do better with me back. And don't you lugs go around talking about what I could do in the post. Eddie is taking over one job, and Lefty Hurst is set in the other. Eddie will start being high-point man before long."

"That will be the day Mister Hurst blows his top," said Buster.

"Let him," said Townsend. "The sooner he realizes we're not a one-man outfit, the better. He may catch on to that this next game."

After an hour Craig called a halt. The other two did not protest; Buster and Eddie were spent, but Moss was highly enthusiastic.

"Much more of this," he gloated, "and I'll be

giving Hurst and Sledge a run for the money. Thanks a lot, Craig. You don't know how much I appreciate your help."

Chapter Seven

Coach Denton could have taken the first Belmont drive as an omen. Sledge tipped the ball up and backward. Craig took possession easily, rising above two Winston opponents. He shot a bouncing pass to Buster, took the ball back immediately. He feinted to Crickett Sledge. At once Winston revealed its defensive pattern for this gangling threat. A forward, Jim Paxton, "slid off" to help center James Maloney cover the slot.

That left Eddie Moss open momentarily. Craig fed him. Moss whirled and drove for the goal. But he was too eager; the ball wobbled on his fingertips. Maloney took possession, and the Wildcats formed deliberately for another attack.

The Wildcats moved the ball carefully. Craig, intent on covering his man, realized they faced an offensive very much along the pattern of Gil Wayne's system. This Winston five would not score too heavily, but they would make few mistakes. Maloney drove in for a crip after drawing Crickett out of position.

Craig took the ball downcourt. So far Coach Denton had shown no preference for either a zone or a man-to-man defense. A good basketball team must know both and be able to change patterns at the coach's signal. Should Craig suggest to Coach Denton that Belmont go into the zone? He decided against it. He must not show too much leadership too soon.

Frank Hurst called for the ball. Craig fed it in, but a split second too late. Frank saw that he was blocked by another sliding defensive maneuver. He threw back to Townsend, and Craig flipped to Moss. The forward leaped too soon, and his basket try was blocked. Winston grabbed the rebound and scored again. Maloney's shot rolled off the hoop, but Jim Paxton broke clear of Hurst to tip in a two-pointer.

Downcourt again, Craig passed up a chance to pass in to Moss. Eddie was trying too hard; let him calm down a bit. Crickett took the floor pass coming in to the post. The tall youth slipped and brushed against Maloney. The referee's whistle nullified Sledge's successful shot. Foul on No. 6. Maloney calmly sank the free try. Winston led 5-0.

The Blue team needed a basket sorely; Craig shifted to Frank. The southpaw ace got his favorite overhanded hook off. It was a wild shot, high on the board, but it swished through the netting in a crazy bounce and counted.

Paxton scored for Winston. Craig led Sledge, and again Crickett fouled. He was overeager, like Eddie Moss. Winston's Chuck Gannaway sank a set shot, and the Wildcats led 9-2.

Coach Denton gestured for a time out. Eddie Moss was replaced by Paul Tipton; Perry took over for Buster. The coach sourly watched this new combination divide baskets with Winston until the score reached 19-12, the Wildcats still leading. Sledge drew his third personal and was forced to play more carefully. Denton rubbed his chin and stared at the maple floor. Crickett and Frank just couldn't carry the scoring load in a two-in attack. Belmont still lacked that third tall boy pushing the boards.

Oh, Frank would get his share of points, all right —when fed the ball. And lean Craig Townsend seemed to sense when the veteran forward was hot. The combination of Craig and Hurst worked furiously for three sensational minutes. Belmont's rooters cheered mightily as the Blue team took the lead. Frank pumped in four field goals and three free tosses. Sledge converted a rebound.

Meanwhile the Wildcat attack lost some of its calm efficiency. Maloney tallied twice; Crickett was too foul-conscious. The score reached 25-22. Jamie Brooks went in for Craig, Eddie returned to the line-up to spell the tiring Hurst. These scoring splurges always left the left-hander exhausted.

Winston tied the score again; Sledge made it 27-25 with a looping hook. There was no doubting this tall boy's possibilities. He would be a great player in a year or two. But now, mused Coach Denton, he was a little ragged about the seams. He couldn't hold James Maloney on defense. The Wildcat center made it 27-27. Ed Barley took the floor and sank a free try to put Belmont one point ahead at intermission.

Coaches Denton and Thomas were not too worried, however. The Wildcats plainly lacked reserve strength. Maloney had not rested for a minute and had three fouls against him. The Winston center wasn't apt to finish the game.

Especially not with Barley and Crickett alternating in the post and pressing alternately. Denton explained his strategy to Craig. Work Maloney hard on defense, tire him out, get him to foul out. Craig nodded. He dropped his eyes to conceal his pleasure. Now he was getting full recognition as the team's strategist.

Barley made good only one of four basket tries, but he drew a foul on Maloney. Crickett returned to action, pressing hard, getting the ball repeatedly. He found easier going as the Wildcat center played him more cautiously. Finally Maloney was relieved with Belmont leading 38-33.

Frank Hurst didn't drop to the floor with his teammates during the timeout.

"Well, Maloney's out a while," the forward said snappishly. "Gimme the ball, Townsend, and let's run up a lead."

"Sure," Craig said lightly. "That's what we've been waiting for."

His eyes gleamed as he slowly brought the ball upcourt. So Mister Hurst didn't quite approve of the Belmont strategy! Well, let him make a basket or two—and stop his sulking. Twice, three times, Frank pumped his fallaway shots into the netting. To the bench he went, then, Belmont leading 49-40. Coach Denton decided to give Craig a rest, too. Brooks and Stanton were holdover starters at the back post. By all rights the Blues should not slack off when this pair took over.

But Jamie and Perry weren't used to feeding Crickett or Eddie Moss. The Belmont attack bogged down. Winston's tight zone held Sledge helpless. Finally the gangling center fouled out. And, with only five minutes left, Jim Maloney returned to the floor. The Wildcat ace scored two quick field goals against the slow, awkward Barley.

Craig edged closer to Coach Denton. "He's eating up Barley on defense. Let me take Maloney."

"Can you handle him?" There was good reason for Denton's hesitancy. Maloney had a five-inch height advantage over Townsend.

"I think so. Barley's doing okay on attack. Let him have Paxton."

Denton nodded. The score was 55-50; obviously he must do something about his defense.

The coach watched closely as Craig took over the defensive post. Twice he leaped high to block basket tries. This product of Gil Wayne's personal coaching packed spring in his well-developed frame. He timed his leaps well, too, getting the most out of his six-feet-three inches.

Maloney was tiring and had four personals against him. He was easier to guard, certainly. But Townsend impressed Denton as capable of checking the Winston ace any time.

And Frank Hurst, rested, getting pass after pass from Townsend, widened the Belmont lead. Denton smiled appreciatively as Craig's strategy showed more plainly. He could hold Maloney; Hurst could hit goals. The combination, plus the moving clock, would save the game for Belmont. The final score was 63-57. The crowd gave the Blue team a spirited ovation as the gun sounded. Belmont had won, and that was the main thing.

But, reflected Coach Denton, his charges had a long way to go. The next game would be played in Winston's gymnasium. The home court advantage would not be overcome easily. He told his players so in the dressing room. They had many a wrinkle to iron out before the next Tuesday night.

✿　✿　✿　✿　✿

Some of the players shared the coach's disgruntled frame of mind. Frank Hurst, for one. He had scored 20 points to confirm his role as Belmont's scoring ace, but he was not completely happy about the way those points had been tallied. It was his feeling that he had fitted into the Blues' offensive picture only as Craig Townsend wished. The Winston defense had never seemed set for him. Given more opportunities, he might have scored twice as many points just as easily.

He confided this feeling to Celeste Petry on their way to the club.

"We could have done a lot better," he complained. "The coach's strategy doesn't make sense to me. All we do is feed Crickett and that Eddie Moss. Sledge is a year away, and I'm not sure Moss will ever make it."

"He did seem to be nervous," nodded the girl. She felt sure that she had a better understanding of the game than most Belmont coeds. Why shouldn't she? She had gone with Frank ever since their junior year in high school. Between her steady and her interested father, she had heard more talk of basketball in these past three years than of any other subject. In fact, she had heard too much of it.

"We could be better than last year," mused Frank. "This Townsend is our best floor man, no doubt about it. If he could learn to work with either Perry or Jamie—and feed me more—"

"Doesn't he work with Perry and Jamie?"

"Not much. He and Tolar team better." Frank scowled at the approaching cars, and eased up on the gas feed. This was Celeste's roadster, but she always insisted that he drive. And she did not like for him to mope along the road, either. What was a sports car for?

"He's a competitor, though," Celeste said knowingly. "It made a difference when Craig guarded that Maloney."

"Sure," grunted Frank. "Maloney was tired. Had four fouls on him, too. Tipton could have handled him those last three minutes, or Kutner."

Celeste studied her date thoughtfully. She was not in love with Frank Hurst, at least she thought she wasn't. She went steady with him because he was handsome, star of the basketball team, a good swimmer, and tennis player. And he was nearly always available. Blessed with a good mind, Frank passed his courses with little effort. Celeste could count on him to accompany her anywhere or any time.

But wasn't he becoming too self-centered? This resentment against Craig Townsend disturbed her. Herbert Petry considered the lean newcomer a valuable asset to the team. "That's what we lacked last year, a good playmaker." Her father had said that several times since the season's opener. And Coach Denton must share the feeling, for there was little doubt that the Blue mentor let Townsend call the turns.

"Don't get jealous, Frank," Celeste said. "Your scoring record isn't everything."

"It's a lot, though," Frank said. "I want a Crown-over scholarship, and those don't come easy."

She tossed her head. "Dad will help you. I'll see to it."

"He'll help—some. But Crownover won't hand out a scholarship just to please your dad. Mr. Petry has said that himself."

"No," admitted Celeste. Her father was an influential alumnus, but the Crownover coaches accepted only about a third of Mr. Petry's recommendations. Coach Millican would personally scout a prospect at her father's request. But Crownover considered and rejected a dozen hopefuls for every one taken.

Celeste stared off into the night. It hadn't occurred to her before that Frank Hurst might not rate a scholarship to her father's alma mater. She was going there herself; Herbert Petry had enrolled his daughter the day after her birth. Had even reserved a room in the college's most exclusive dormitory nineteen years in advance. What if Frank had to accept an offer from another college? That would finish their romance, certainly, for Celeste had no intention of marrying early. Her father wanted her to graduate from Crownover and then travel abroad. The prospect pleased her.

It was something to think about, mused Celeste. Maybe she and her father had overestimated Frank's basketball ability. Certainly his present resentful attitude hurt his future chances.

How different were Craig Townsend's reactions to the game! Craig came to dance with her almost immediately, which pleased Celeste no little. She had not understood his first indifference to her. It had been somewhat challenging to face a Belmont basketball player who wasn't awed by the combination of her looks and her father's position.

"And you can dance, too," she said after a moment. "Didn't the game wear you out?"

The music stopped. Herbert Petry beckoned to his daughter from across the floor. Celeste wondered if Craig hadn't sought out her father yet. Belmont cagers were supposed to do that without delay. They almost always humored this banker who created part-time jobs for their support.

Then Celeste remembered that this lean young man had not asked any favors of Herbert Petry. Craig Townsend had come to Belmont strictly on his own.

"Nice game, Townsend," Mr. Petry said warmly as the young couple joined him. "We had our anxious moments, but we got by with it."

"They gave us trouble," nodded Craig. "We aren't too ready."

"I thought that myself," Mr. Petry said a bit grimly. "The club has fine possibilities but seems to be slow coming around. What do you think is the trouble?"

"None," Craig said calmly. "We're working toward a well-rounded attack, that's all. Moss is inexperienced, Sledge is still a little clumsy. But we've nothing to worry about. There's still Frank."

Mr. Petry lit a cigar, his eyes studying Townsend. "Is that it? We're trying to get away from a one-man team?"

"Sort of. But Frank is still our best basket bet."

Celeste liked his quick but casual praise of a teammate. How different was this attitude from Frank's!

"You should make more points yourself, son," said Mr. Petry. "The baskets are the main thing."

"Yes, sir," said Craig with a smile. "I suppose the difference is that I don't care who makes the baskets, just so they count for us."

"Well, you'll never get into the doghouse with that attitude," approved Mr. Petry.

Her father, decided Celeste, was liking Craig Townsend more all the time. She wasn't sure that she didn't feel the same way.

* * * * *

Officially the Belmont squad had the weekend off. But Crickett Sledge, Buster Tolar, and Eddie Moss worked overtime—and under a sterner task-master than Coach Forrest Denton.

"It's up to you guys," Craig told them. "I can still remember how Gil Wayne coached me. He worked me until my tongue hung out. Some nights I had to drag myself off the floor. We went over my mistakes until I quit making so many of them. I'll work with you if you say so. But the word is work."

The trio pledged their best efforts. They took Craig's sarcasm without resentment. Getting Crickett and Eddie to loosen up was the hardest part.

"Let your playmaker do the thinking," advised Townsend. "Your back is to the defense. Don't think about the man guarding you. Get set—flick a signal to Buster—"

He showed them what he meant, with Buster to throw and Sledge to guard him. Tolar shot in a bouncing pass to Craig's left. He took the ball with one hand as he went up into the air. Whirl and shoot with the same motion, he told the two tall players.

"That way you get the break on fouls," he explained. "But if you're blocked—"

He showed Tolar how to follow up a pass. The playmaker should move to position to cover a backward flip from the hard-pressed post man.

"Don't take time to look," Craig said. "Go up, get off the shot if you can, but get rid of the ball anyhow. Don't worry about your guard's being ready for the pass. I'll be there every time. So will Buster—even if we have to bend ax handles over his head."

Ball control at close quarters, that was Gil Wayne's system. Protect the ball at all times. Craig could do it. An arched shoulder, the upraised bent arm—Crickett shook his head ruefully. Any physical contact found Craig defending the ball with shoulder or bent elbow.

"Sort of like in-fighting," explained Townsend, "though I'm no boxer. And get off a shot at contact —any kind of shot. You got to be something of a ham actor. All you're doing is hooking for the basket as you try to pull away from the man guarding you. Remember to be pulling back."

Both Crickett and Eddie were slow to protect the ball. Craig took turns guarding each. Time after time he eluded their shields to slap the basketball. Grimly, Sledge and Moss kept trying.

"You play rough," sighed Moss. Craig had just jolted the ball out of his hands. "I'd hate to have you on me in a regular game."

"I wouldn't be this rough," conceded Craig. "I'm trying to get you used to contact. It won't hurt you to be bumped and elbowed. The thing is to hold the ball anyhow. You can learn to make baskets with two men draped all over you."

They had paused to catch their breath. "I guess we've copied Frank's style," said Crickett. "We're used to getting clear before we shoot."

"And to shooting every time you go up," nodded Craig. "That's the Hurst style, all right. He's good with that fallaway shot. But he misses half the time, anyhow. Any forward does. And the ball is lost if he doesn't hit."

Craig spent almost as much time with Tolar. Buster wasn't accustomed to such passing responsibility. Right or left, high or low, bounce or lob, the decision was his. Also the obligation of retrieving any loose-bouncing ball. "Your post man is going up and away," lectured Craig. "If the ball is knocked loose, it will go behind and to the outside. Be there to get it or at least tie up the other team. When you get the ball, dribble for the corner. Your middle out man—"

He showed what he meant. That was his favorite role. The guard going into the corner should know where to look for his teammate. The other post man should break for the basket. The ball exchange must be quick and sure. It worked often enough for Buster and Eddie to learn their respective assignments. Crickett, too—for the pivot man was not through when the ball left his possession. He was to screen for the pass exchange between Buster and Craig. Crickett was not to wait, then, to see what would happen. He was to go up on the boards in anticipation of Eddie's quick basket try.

"You can't wait to see what the guards will do," Craig pointed out. "Pivot men don't think. They're in there for the height. You're playing because you're nearly seven feet tall. That height won't help if you're standing flat-footed. Be up for every rebound."

"But what if Eddie can't get off his shot?" objected Sledge.

"That's his worry," shrugged Craig. "Sure he won't be free all the time. But if that's all he's thinking about while Buster takes the ball and throws to me, he'll be loose more times than not. And you'll be up on the rim, too. The instant the ball gets away from you, get up there. Slide around the guy guarding you."

Craig's eyes twinkled. "Just keep working," he encouraged. "You'll see results before long. That's the way pros play the game. That's why their scores run so high. There's no stopping their attack except with a tight zone, a real tight one. And the pros ruled out that kind of defense to make the game more interesting."

"Golly, golly," sighed Buster. "I never saw anybody work at a game like you do."

"I had to," Craig said slowly. "It's the only way I can get a college education and prepare myself to be anything except a section hand or a truck driver."

His gray eyes moved from one to the other. "I play the game hard," he said slowly. "You don't have to play it my way. I'm working with you because you asked me."

"Sure," Buster said quickly. "And we'll play your way. We like it."

Eddie nodded. Crickett Sledge hesitated.

"You're the one with the most to gain, Sledge," Craig said tersely. "If I had your reach, I'd be the best post man in college basketball next year."

"You would be," the gangling youth conceded. He smiled ruefully. "You're the best I ever played against as it is. I've learned something this weekend. It wasn't an accident the way you bottled up Maloney. And I don't know what would happen if you ever moved in to the post and hogged the shots like Frank Hurst."

"That won't happen," promised Craig. "I could rack up some points, sure. But who's satisfied to be a big frog in a little puddle?"

*   *   *   *   *

Coach Forrest Denton quickly appreciated the improvement in Tolar, Sledge, and Moss. The Blue mentor tested a new starting combination: Hurst and Stanton as forwards, Barley as center, Craig and Brooks as out men. Perry Stanton and Jamie Brooks were holdover starters; Denton wanted to include them in any first-string combination. And with Townsend coming on so rapidly, what else could he do but try Stanton in the front line?

That scrimmage setup put Moss and Crickett in the double post with Tolar as their playmaker. Craig could have stymied their maneuvers. Why not? They were using the tricks he had taught them Saturday and Sunday. But he carefully performed the defensive duties assigned him, to guard Stanton. Let Hurst and Barley stop the improved Crickett and Moss if they could, and Jamie Brooks heckle Buster's playmaking.

The three newcomers had learned their first lessons well. At first, it seemed to Coach Denton that the lanky Sledge was playing indifferently. He'd go up with the ball, lob it backward. Buster seemed to be there every time, but the coach didn't realize immediately that this was calm ball-handling, not just young Tolar's hustle. And Tolar's dribble into the corner, his throws to Kutner, the breaks under the basket by Eddie Moss!

Time after time Denton blew his whistle to stop the scrimmage. "Moss is getting open," he snapped at Kutner. "You're not seeing him."

97

Mark nodded ruefully. He began flipping to Eddie. The forward missed his hook more often than not. But Crickett Sledge was up on the rim for any loose, rolling ball. The scrimmage turned out to be a ding-dong battle. Carefully Craig kept his feelings to himself. And he made no move to leave his own opponent to block those delayed rushes. He wanted Eddie and Buster to win first-string assignments. Sledge would, for sure. Coaches took a beanpole and played him for better or for worse, trusting that experience would smooth out the rough spots. But Moss and Tolar had hills to climb. Both coaches were reluctant to give up on Stanton and Brooks.

The starting line-up included both as Belmont moved in on Winston. This second clash with the Wildcats would make or break the Blues as a championship outfit. Belmont had barely won in its own gymnasium. Wouldn't the going be rougher on the Winston maples? Jim Maloney might go wild on a more familiar backboard.

Forrest Denton had a possible solution for Maloney. The coach took a quarter hour to pattern a special defense for the Wildcat center. Craig would slide off his man to check Maloney's sweeps to his right. Sledge would not press his man too hard. The Blue beanpole would drop back to take rebounds, leaving Townsend to struggle with Maloney's pivot.

Craig's eyes gleamed approval. "I'll handle him," he promised. He said that without braggadocio. "He's taller, but I can beat him off the floor when he starts up. He won't hit 60 per cent of his shots tonight."

Denton smothered his sigh. Apparently this lean newcomer had already figured out such a defensive move himself. The coach was left with the feeling that Townsend had already decided to give Sledge a jump on the defensive post.

The tip went to the Wildcats. Winston's usual roll sent the pass in to Maloney. He feinted to his left, pulling over Sledge. The Winston center then swung out to his own right, going up for his hook shot. Coach Denton had observed that Maloney favored right-handed hooks. He wasn't nearly so deadly from the port side.

Craig Townsend partially deflected the shot. It fell short and into the waiting hands of Crickett Sledge. The beanpole slumped to his knees, shielding the ball with both elbows. Deliberately he pitched back to Craig. Denton nodded in approval. He was glad that Sledge was learning to protect the ball at all costs.

But Frank missed his basket try downcourt, and

the Wildcats took possession. Hurst had hurried his shot, no doubt about it. Seldom could Frank score in the early seconds, but Coach Denton made no move to send in a substitute even after another wild try. He had confidence in Frank's point-making ability. Who didn't? This slim southpaw had averaged over twenty points per game since his sophomore year in high school.

Belmont's sliding defense was holding Maloney; that was the big thing. And Sledge rolled in a crip to put Belmont ahead. Crickett sank two free tries, and Perry Stanton sank a two-hander from back of the circle. Coach Denton frowned despite the 6-0 lead. Perry should be working for the boards, not shooting from the circle. Stanton might as well forget his out man's role, as far as this season was concerned, anyhow. He had been a capable playmaker the season before, but now this cool, businesslike Townsend was in charge, very much in charge.

The double responsibility on defense didn't phase Townsend. Jamie Brooks, noticed Denton, was stalling the Blue attack until Craig was in position. In just three weeks Jamie had surrendered leadership to the newcomer.

Hurst hit a fallaway and Winston retaliated with two quick baskets. Maloney didn't make them. The Wildcat pivot man threw off to his teammates, and the two teams traded baskets until the score reached 14-7. Maloney was a basketball player. Tie him up and he would pass off. The leaks in Belmont's defense were Hurst and Stanton. Frank had never been anything but a so-so guard. Perry was taking slowly to his new assignment.

Coach Denton sent in Eddie and Buster. Off came Jamie, who had performed well. The coach said so. Belmont was not hurting in the back court any time. If Sledge improved, if Denton found a third up-man—those two solutions would satisfy Denton.

He watched closely as the quartet of Eddie, Craig, Buster, and Crickett sped up the pace. To the average eye it appeared that Townsend figured little in these assaults on the Winston basket. But Coach Denton was not fooled, nor was the Wildcat mentor. It was not by accident that the capable Maloney found himself screened time and time again. Townsend set the play in motion and moved carefully to a spot on the floor where he inconvenienced Maloney the most.

Sledge up for two points, Eddie in for two baskets in a row, Crickett calmly slapping in a rebound as Moss missed. In just 120 seconds the score reached 22-9, and Winston called time out. The Blue cheering section roared an ovation for the five players

kneeling around their gray-haired coach: OUR TEAM
IS RED HOT!

Denton agreed. This offensive flurry had shocked
him a little. He had not expected such improvement in either Moss or Tolar. He slapped both boys
on the shoulder.

"Keep it up," he encouraged. "Frank, I'll rest
you a while. Let these kids have their fling."

Perry returned to the court. He did not fit into
this driving attack much better than Hurst. But
he would pass the ball off; Craig and Buster were
willing to use him more. Winston's strategy changed,
too. The Wildcats eased the pressure on Maloney.
Two guards started pumping one-handers at the
basket. Perry fitted better than Frank into the
changing Belmont defense. Stanton moved quicker
to heckle set shooters.

With five minutes left the score stood 34-18.
Coach Denton rubbed his chin in satisfaction, then
sent in Hurst, Barley, Brooks, and Tipton. He liked
to be able to make such substitutions; any coach
did.

Frank Hurst knew these teammates well, and they
knew him. So far the star Belmont forward had
tallied only three points. Grimly he set out to make
up for lost time. His inevitable hot streak was due;
it came. He took seven of his fallaway shots in

those next five minutes. Five times the ball swished through the netting. He converted two out of three tries from the foul line. He had fifteen points to his personal credit as the half ended with Belmont leading 51-24. The Blue supporters screamed in ecstasy as Coach Denton led his charges to the dressing room. What was this about the home team having an advantage?

※　※　※　※　※

Coach Denton did not believe in running up crushing totals against outclassed opponents. He believed in using all his players when the score allowed. He allowed Jamie, Perry, Kutner, and Barley to play most of the second half. The unit of Hurst, Craig, Buster, Crickett, and Eddie got only five minutes of action. This combination still clicked but not as sensationally as in the first half, for Winston tightened its patrol of the post. Hurst and Buster scored two baskets each from back of the circle, but Coach Denton saw enough to confirm his feeling that his ideas about a starting line-up must be revised. Then he called Craig and Sledge to the side lines for the remainder of the game.

Frank Hurst liked the closely-drawn Wildcat defense. This was something new in his experience—

a defense designed to stop his teammates. He racked up five quick baskets before the Wildcats returned to their original pattern.

Denton relieved the star forward for a few minutes, then returned him to the floor. The coach had learned the hard way about Frank Hurst. He must be played into physical condition. He would not follow a strenuous training program. He would play hard in a game, play himself to a frazzle. The only way to condition him for full-time action was to keep him playing.

The score was 69-30 when Hurst returned after his rest. Frank immediately showed his intention to break his individual scoring record. He had tallied 34 points in one game his first season. With still a minute and eight seconds left, he tied that mark.

He missed a fallaway, picked himself up quickly, scrambled to steal the ball from Winston's Cliff Mabry. Panting, wobbling, Frank drove downcourt alone. Two Wildcats raced to intercept him. They blocked his way to the basket, but Frank had no intention of passing back to a teammate. The seconds were ticking off; he must make this basket himself. He feinted to his left, swung on his pivot foot, twisting his body backward. He leaped high enough to get off his jump shot. He thudded to the maples as the ball swished through the netting.

Pain paralyzed him as he tried to rise. Perry realized he had an injury and appealed to the referee, who signaled an official time out.

Frank struggled erect. He had turned his left ankle, the one which bore most of the strain of his hook shot. He was able to hobble off the floor with Perry's assistance. The gymnasium literally shook with applause for the injured player. A new individual scoring record for the Lone Star Junior-College Conference! That's what he had accomplished with this desperate leap. Wildcat supporters joined in the demonstration, too.

But neither his coach nor his teammates echoed the enthusiasm. Twisted ankle! How bad? The conference battles came thick and fast now—a two-game series every week. How long would Frank be out?

The Belmont physician who doubled as team trainer shook his head. He did not know. He was sure there wasn't a break, though he would order X rays. It looked as if Frank would be ready again in a couple of weeks.

A couple of weeks! That took most of the joy out of this smashing 86-47 victory. What a fool stunt, Coach Denton groaned to himself! He was chiefly to blame; he should not have let Frank play so long.

But he had not felt like pulling the forward out of the game with a scoring record so near.

Craig Townsend had driven to Winston in his own car. Mary, Buster, and Eddie had accompanied him; they added Crickett Sledge to their number as they started home.

"Oh, I hope Frank isn't out too long," worried Mary. "You had just started clicking tonight."

"Oh, we won't miss Frank so much," said Buster. "Coach Craig there keeps us humping."

"Your charges are improving, Craig," said Mary. "Buster especially. We don't know how to thank you."

"Forget it," shrugged Craig. "I need a guard to team with me."

Her eyes studied his lean face. "Why not Perry or Jamie? Everybody was sure they would play first string. Then you came along—and now it's Buster."

"Would they have worked with me like Buster has? Or Frank Hurst, would he?" Craig grinned. "They would resent my trying to show them anything. You've got to be hungry to learn much."

"Not everybody," said Mary. "You have a hard creed, Mr. Townsend."

"Maybe, but it gets results." He shifted his weight under the steering wheel. "We got results tonight.

We'll sweep both games with Lafayette even with Hurst out. Eddie and Crickett can pick up the slack."

"Do you dislike Frank?"

"Why, no. Why should I?"

"I just wondered."

"Look, Mary," Craig said patiently, "I don't care who makes the points or who gets the headlines."

"You make that very clear," she said slowly.

"What do you mean?"

"Everybody's talking about it—how you try to shift credit to the other boys. But you make something else pretty plain, too. The team falls apart without you."

Craig suppressed his smile. He really created that strong an impression in so short a time? Did the spectators actually realize who carried the load for undefeated Belmont on both offense and defense? If so, then Herbert Petry was surely aware of it, and also the university scouts studying every box score of this fast junior-college conference. Craig Townsend sighed. He had accomplished a great deal in these last few weeks. He was off scholastic probation. He had made a flying start toward an athletic scholarship. And he had overcome his shyness and mingled well with his fellow students. He shot a sidewise glance at Mary Tolar.

Wasn't it time he relaxed his grim schedule and allowed himself more social life? He could afford to spend a little money. He was a full hundred dollars under the budget he had allowed himself for the year.

"Do you have a date tomorrow night?"

His abrupt question startled Mary. She had been wondering if Craig Townsend had some sort of hesitancy about dating a teammate's sister.

"Why, no," she said after a moment.

"Am I eligible?"

"I suppose so. I don't know of any reason why not."

"Then how about it?"

She hesitated. Was it such a serious decision? Her lips tightened. It wasn't to her, for something warned her that Craig Townsend might prove just as intent about this as about everything else.

"All right," she said casually. "Stop by the library after basketball practice."

*　*　*　*　*

Another private automobile took the injured Frank Hurst back to Belmont. Its driver was not in a happy humor. Celeste had a good reason for disliking to drive on the highway. She was nearsighted but had refused stubbornly to wear either glasses or contact lenses. She gave a light, stock answer to all suggestions about either: boys didn't make passes at girls who wore glasses.

She usually turned the wheel of her convertible over to Frank, especially at night. But the star forward could not drive with his right ankle heavily wrapped with gauze and adhesive tape.

"You had the game sewed up," she said crossly. "There was no point in driving yourself so hard."

"I wanted that record," shrugged Frank. "I may not be that hot again this season." A happy smile formed on his face. "I was really hitting them. No telling what I would have scored if Townsend had fed me more."

"He mixes up the attack," Celeste said, repeating her father's statement. "Crickett and Eddie are coming along. No use of our having a one-man attack."

"I guess not," agreed Hurst. But his scowl showed that he was not pleased with sharing basket-making duties. "But Sledge and Moss haven't clicked against the tough teams yet. Wait till we hit Warmouth and Hampton."

"What about Lafayette? You'll miss both games."

"We might squeak by. But the out men must

shoot more. And Townsend can't hit like Perry or Jamie."

"How do you know he can't? He appears to be capable of doing whatever is required of him."

"Yeah, he's a cool cat," snapped Frank. "Good dancer, too. Maybe you ought to latch on to him while I'm laid up."

"Don't tempt me," Celeste said with a cool smile. "He's a fine hunk of man. He's been around."

"Sure, greasing airplanes. Doing KP duty. But you're a little late, Bright Eyes. Mary Tolar has already hooked him."

That was the wrong thing to say. Celeste Petry liked challenges. She laid her head back against the leather upholstery and drove slowly. Her relationship with Mary Tolar had always been a cool one. Polite, yes, but with a mutual distrust. Mary had been plain and dumpy in her early teens. Celeste had never found her a rival, but Mary grew more attractive every year. Celeste had made mental note of that the previous summer. Maybe, she mused, this dark-haired assistant librarian should be showed that Celeste could still take her pick of Belmont's male students.

Chapter Eight

The Blues' weekend game was a non-conference clash with St. Ignatius, a Catholic academy. At least, reflected Coach Denton, he would have an opportunity to experiment freely with a new front-line combination. St. Ignatius lacked the height and reserves to menace Belmont's unbeaten record.

The coach started Perry and Moss as forwards. The former would not develop into a hard board worker, but Stanton had a good shooting eye. He could hit from the corner especially. And Forrest Denton was almost convinced that he must use a variation of the double post. And two newcomers, Eddie and Crickett, must carry the full load.

Townsend and Jamie Brooks at guards—the coach was still reluctant to promote Buster Tolar to a starting assignment. Certainly the skinny towhead was improving. He would play quite a bit this season, to spell off either guard. Or would the coach rest Craig at all in close games? Denton was not sure.

The conference season was half over, and the coach already regarded Craig as almost irreplaceable. Against St. Ignatius, yes. Coach Denton relieved Craig and Crickett after five minutes of play. Belmont had a 14-2 lead already, and the Blue combination was sure to widen the gap. The coach seized the opportunity to give Ed Barley more experience in the post. A championship team needed two towering centers. The taller the player, the more likely he was to foul out. Already Belmont had felt the pinch when five personals took their pivot man out of the line-up. Townsend had saved their hides by guarding Jim Maloney with almost uncanny efficiency. Craig could probably repeat that trick, too.

But Coach Denton was reluctant to place any more responsibility on Townsend. Why? The mentor didn't understand his own feelings about his lean, rangy playmaker. Why should he resent Craig's cool assumption of team leadership? Why should it secretly aggravate him that Craig persistently ignored the play combinations which would have sent him in to the basket? Townsend knew his job. He knew the game better than any other young player Denton had ever watched. This alert, businesslike performer was a great credit to Gilbert Wayne's coaching. Did that rankle Forrest Denton? He could not take personal pride in Craig's prowess. All the Belmont coach had done was to allow a new student to try out for the team. He would have allowed any other youth the same privilege. One practice session, just a few minutes of one practice, and cool Craig Townsend had won a varsity berth.

The margin over St. Ignatius widened. Denton ran his ten players in and out but allowed Eddie Moss to dominate the scoring. The development of another backboard threat was vital to the Blues' championship hopes. Eddie had the height, six-feet-four inches of it. He was speedy, too, if a little slow in his reactions. He would make a fine forward in his second season, no doubt of it. But what about this year? Could Eddie elude good guarding?

He was improving in every game. Three weeks ago Denton had not seriously considered the black-haired boy as a possible starter. Now the coach dared to hope that Moss might be the answer to his offensive worries.

Eddie marked up 28 points as Belmont coasted to an 81-42 victory. Sledge scored 20 points despite only nine minutes of play. Crickett's total did not confirm any improvement, however. He had simply risen up over the heads of his smaller opponents and pushed the ball in.

But Moss—he had showed signs of more aggressiveness and better ball-handling. Denton asked the black-haired forward to stay after the others were gone.

"You're coming along, son," the coach said warmly. "You started out as if you wouldn't make the grade this year."

Eddie Moss beamed. "Yes, sir. I don't lose the ball going up as I did. I'm still shaky on defense, but I'm working on it."

Denton nodded. Eddie could still be fooled by a clever charge. "I understand you're putting in extra time. You, Crickett, Tolar, and Townsend."

"Yes, sir. Every weekend." Eddie shook his dark head ruefully. "Townsend puts us through the mill. Works us on our individual weaknesses. He swears he'll make a good defensive hand out of me or kill me. I suppose he will, too." Moss grinned. "I know this, if I can ever stop him on the boards, I'll hold anybody in this league."

"On the boards? You mean driving for the basket?"

"Yes, sir. He's rough, Coach. Crickett and I double up on him, and he still gets up on the rim."

Coach Denton rubbed his chin thoughtfully. For

some reason this bit of information didn't shock him. He did not find it surprising that Craig Townsend could take care of himself at close quarters under the post. Denton well remembered Gil Wayne's crack college outfits. Every man in the starting line-up had been a threat to charge the boards.

"Well," Denton said a little weakly, "keep it up. You'll make a basketball player yet."

He didn't add what he was thinking—that Craig Townsend would deserve personal credit for this development, too.

*　*　*　*　*

Lafayette had lost two close decisions to Winston. The Blues would have been a strong favorite to win the series if it had not been for Hurst's injury. As it was, the sports writers rated the two games as toss ups. The Belmont student body feared that their team would have a hard time staying on the unbeaten list, especially in Lafayette's gym. And particularly was the first game a crucial test. Within five minutes Coach Denton realized that Crickett Sledge carried their victory hopes. Lafayette's Carl Bronson could check Eddie's basket rushes. And a pint-sized speedster named Tack Collins bothered Stanton's shots from the corner. Jamie sank two straight jump shots from outside the circle; those baskets represented the 14-10 difference as Lafayette called time out.

Coach Denton talked over strategy changes with his perspiring charges. "Try to get open some," he told Craig. "Your man is falling off to help on Sledge."

Townsend nodded. He had realized that, but he felt sure that the tall Crickett would wear down the visitors' post defense eventually. The gangling center was gaining in physical endurance as well as smoothness and self-confidence. To Craig's way of thinking, this series offered the chance to develop Sledge as a full-time scoring threat.

And now, too, was the chance to prove that Belmont could win without Frank Hurst. Craig smiled to himself as he stood up and studied two replacements in the Lafayette line-up. The home team relieved Tom Perkins, its tall center. His substitute was as rangy but looked to be more clumsy. Craig slapped Crickett's shoulder as play resumed. Sledge was rested after the time out; the new Lafayette center might be sluggish from sitting on the bench. Basketball players didn't get to warm up like baseball pitchers.

"You got a new pal," Craig smiled. "Let's see how he ticks."

Buster had replaced Jamie during the rest. Craig bounced the ball over to Tolar and gestured to Eddie. Buster dribbled across court. This was another of their private patterns. Slow-starting at first. Buster innocently passed in to Moss. Eddie half turned as if intending to drive for the hoop. He was blocked out. He threw back to Craig. Across court came Buster at full speed. Those next two passes would be quick. Craig flipped to Tolar and moved along the keyhole. Buster shot a bouncing pass to Crickett. The tall center feinted to his right, then whirled. A green-shirted guard was supposed to cover this maneuver, but Craig stood squarely in the way. Sledge brushed against Townsend but went up for his shot anyhow. It swished through the hoop, and the referee whistled a personal foul against Lafayette to boot. The new Green center had tried to recover position and had fouled Crickett after the shot.

Sledge converted the free throw, and Belmont led 17-10. But the visitors quickly tallied two points. Sledge got free for a crip shot, with Buster providing the screen this time. Coach Denton shook his head and shot Jamie Brooks a pitying sidewise glance. Jamie was a hard-working veteran who had looked forward to closing out his junior-college career in fine style. But this eager, speedy Tolar kid was proving a better player. He teamed with Townsend like clockwork. He and Craig could work in the ball better than any other Blue combination in recent years. They fed Crickett with unerring precision. The tall center's steady tide of baskets held a ten-point margin over the steady efforts of the Lafayette players. The green-shirted team did not have a strong keyhole attack, but its guards could hit from the outside. There was no playing a zone defense against Lafayette; the Blue cagers had to take the opposition man for man.

And that was telling on Crickett as the half neared its end. Lafayette used three different centers. As soon as one showed signs of tiring, another lumbered in. They are trying to wear Crickett out, sighed Denton, to make him foul. The coach sent Barley in to allow his pivot man a breathing spell. Promptly, Perkins—the Lafayette starter—returned to the floor. He tallied five quick points, too, as the slower, clumsier Barley was unable to handle him. Belmont called for a time out, and Crickett returned to action. The alarmed Belmont fans roared whole-hearted approval. The score was 24-20. This Blue team had to have Sledge and no doubt about it. He had tallied 15 of Belmont's points so far.

Lafayette's strategy was quickly apparent. The Green team speeded up its attack. Let Bob Parrish and Chuck Elliott pepper the Blue basket from outside, and Perkins press hard for the rebounds. That kept Crickett going up on the rim repeatedly, forcing him into body contact with the opposing center. A foul was called after nearly every rebound, mostly against Perkins. He had four before the half ended. There were some against Crickett, too. And Lafayette could replace Perkins. If the two pivot men fouled each other out, Belmont would suffer. Denton looked sadly at Frank Hurst, watching the game glumly from the bench. Oh, how they could use one of Frank's typical scoring sprees now! Belmont held its lead until the gun. The margin of 36-30 was no mean one, and Sledge personally had accounted for nineteen of those points. Could he keep up that pace to the finish?

The Blue cagers were worried, Moss especially. "What am I doing wrong, Coach? That Bronson is handcuffing me. Stays right on top of me."

"Nothing wrong," Denton said tersely. "He's a good boy, that's all. We're just up against what I expected without Frank. Bronson is keeping you out of the keyhole. That leaves us one man going up for baskets. Stanton, you got to go in on the boards. You, too, Townsend. You're doing a fine job of setting up plays and screening for Crickett, but we need more than that."

"We sure do," agreed Craig. "I'll go in when I see an opening. But won't we get better results with the other forward coming in? Buster and I can set up openings for him."

The coach frowned. Why was Townsend assuming that Tolar would play the other guard position most of this half? Coach Denton hadn't thought much about it, but he had rather expected to return Jamie to the line-up.

"We'll try it," Denton nodded. "Either you or Perry must help on the boards."

Stanton tried manfully. Tolar and Craig made good efforts to clear him, too. Coach Denton was sure of both things. But he was equally sure, after six minutes of the second half, that Perry wasn't getting the job done. Nearly all of his experience had been in the back court. This business of driving for the rim was new to him, and baffling.

Regretfully, Denton sent in Mark Kutner. Now, reflected the coach, he didn't have a single hold-over in the game. He had known only two of the five boys on the court before the start of this season. He had handpicked Sledge and Kutner from the high-school ranks, planning a starting role for one and relief assignments for the other. Townsend, Tolar, Moss—who would have predicted in November that Belmont would be risking its conference lead on their performances? Certainly not the Belmont coach.

But it was his most successful combination yet; Denton could not deny that. Kutner fought hard to reach the rim. He made only one basket in those next three minutes, but his aggressiveness occupied a Green defender full time and thus eased the pressure on Sledge. Up went the tall center, twice to score field goals, and to convert free tries as the various Lafayette centers guarded him too closely.

With fourteen minutes left, the Blues led 39-31. The persistent outshooters kept the Green players in the game. No doubt about it, this would be a ding-dong battle to the finish.

Denton talked to his players during a time out, returned to his chair. He sat down just as Frank Hurst asked the student manager about Crickett Sledge's point total.

"Twenty-six," came the answer.

Coach Denton frowned. He had not realized that the pivot man was so near to the conference individual scoring record. But why not, he mused. Wasn't the Belmont attack concentrating on Crickett's shooting?

The referee's whistle stopped a scramble under the Lafayette basket. Denton rose quickly. The foul was against one of his players; he could be sure of that. He groaned as the official identified the Blue defender. Sledge!

The coach gestured to Ed Barley. What else was there to do? Let Crickett rest a few minutes, then return for as long as he could play.

Craig came over to the bench. Perkins was returning to the Lafayette line-up.

"Want me to take him on defense?" Townsend asked.

Denton hesitated, then nodded. "You'd better." For there was little doubt in his mind that Craig was the better guard despite Barley's height.

Two minutes later Denton sent in Stanton for Barley. Craig was guarding Perkins tightly. Lafayette had narrowed the Belmont lead to 43-36, but the Greens were scoring from the outside. Perry would do a better job against such shooting, and the gangling Ed Barley was not penetrating the tight Lafayette zone defense. Stanton was a dependable player even if he couldn't make a showing on the rims.

This combination worked. Denton approved of the way Townsend held his teammates to a deliberate pace on the attack. That reflected Gil Wayne's training, too, mused the Blue coach. Wayne's teams had always been noted for controlling the tempo of a game.

His lean face never showed it, but Craig was getting more and more concerned. Lafayette brought the score to 49-45. A four-point lead wasn't much against a club with two dependable set shooters. Craig whispered instructions to Buster. The Blue guards switched to patterns which allowed Perry to shoot from his favorite corner. Eddie Moss got away from his defender and drove in for a layup. The score stood 57-52 with six minutes left to play. And Crickett Sledge rose at his coach's gesture and stripped off his sweat suit.

Craig said something to Crickett as the tall boy came onto the court. Denton realized the guard's instructions a few seconds later. Townsend meant to keep on defending against Lafayette's various pivot men. Let Crickett be spared any rugged defense work.

The sudden switch in tempo caught Lafayette napping. In one second Belmont moved carefully and deliberately on attack; the next instant Buster and Craig were moving and passing on the dead run. Three straight baskets by the refreshed Sledge resulted. The score reached 63-55. And with three minutes to go, gangling Crickett Sledge was very much a threat to Frank Hurst's scoring mark. The gymnasium buzzed with a fresh wave of excitement.

Then, as abruptly, playmaker Townsend slowed

down his team again. Coach Denton shook his head in admiration. This lean guard didn't need steadying advice from a coach. Nor was he at a disadvantage against Lafayette's taller Perkins. What he lacked in reach he made up with near flawless timing. And his endurance—after these thirty-eight minutes of grueling play, he could still shift quickly to check any Green drive for the basket. Yes, sir, mused Denton, Townsend was a great court man. And Eddie Moss claimed that he was a master at driving for the basket, too! Why did he refuse to go up for his share of the points? Had he deliberately let down every time Denton tried him in a forward's role? Denton sighed and wished he could get to know his new star better. But how could he manage that? Who did know Craig Townsend? Probably Buster, Crickett, and Eddie thought they did, but Coach Denton doubted it.

Feed Sledge! Give it to Crickett! The Belmont fans pleaded for the Blue cagers to give Crickett a fair chance at a new scoring record. But Craig and the others ignored their chants; so did Crickett. The ball shot from Townsend to Perry to Buster. Stanton fitted well into this ball-handling setup. He was an expert dribbler, and this skill set up an opening under the basket. Perry fired a pass in to Crickett, and the rangy center reached up and laid the ball in the basket.

One minute and five seconds left! Craig called time out, but the Blue team didn't come to the bench. They formed a strategy of their own. Crickett stayed under the Lafayette goal as the Green cagers went down to attack. No Belmont player tried to stop a goal. Quickly Buster threw downcourt to Craig. In went a pass to Sledge. Up leaped his shot. Off the rim it rolled. But a blue-jerseyed figure snatched the ball away from two green-shirted players. Townsend up on the board, controlling the rebound! Back went the ball to Tolar. The slight guard held it only an instant. Sledge had the ball again. Townsend was screening for him on one side and Eddie Moss on the other. The tall center stumbled in his determination. But he got off a shot as he lurched sideways and forward. A hoarse roar sounded from every throat in the gymnasium. The shot was good! Crickett Sledge had set a new individual scoring record!

Lafayette scored again to make the final count 67-59. Crickett slumped weakly to the floor as the gun sounded, completely spent. But a grin covered his face from ear to ear.

"Thanks, Craig," he gulped. "Thanks a million."

Coach Denton stood up with a sigh. Delighted

Belmont supporters were all over the court; Denton couldn't have reached Sledge if he had tried. He felt like yelling at the top of his lungs himself. This had been a tough one. Lafayette should be easier on the Belmont floor. And Hurst would be in the line-up the following week.

Coach Denton looked to see how Frank was taking this acclaim for Crickett Sledge. The forward was bearing up pretty well, decided Denton. Actually he was a fine kid, never as cocky and self-centered as he sometimes seemed. He rather hated to see his name wiped off the record books, of course. Who wouldn't? And he'll never get it back there, thought the Blue coach, for Belmont would never depend as much on Frank's fallaway shots again. The Blues had a playmaker now who didn't risk any player's brilliance, not even his own.

*　　*　　*　　*　　*

"That game turned out just right," Denton told his players. "We were lucky enough to win it, and we needed that. We need to sweep this series and then beat Calumet two straight. If we haven't lost any when we get to Warmouth and Hampton, we'll stand some chance. Just a chance, mind you. Don't let what we've done so far go to your heads. Hampton and Warmouth are still the big guns in this league. We're not up to either one yet, but we're coming along, and hard work might get us there."

He paused for breath. "Now let's get some good out of this game. What did we lack last night besides Frank? We didn't have three men up on the boards. Eddie was tied up all night. I don't blame him too much. Bronson is a good guard. But you gave up too easily, Moss, and you know it."

Eddie dropped his head guiltily. "I'll give him more trouble Friday night," he promised.

"You'd better," Denton said crisply. "Now, you, Perry. Are you going to make a forward or not?" The coach rather hated to single out Stanton so sharply. The veteran was trying a role he had never filled before and had never expected to play. "If you're not," continued Denton, "we had better use three out and two in until Frank can play again. You just raced your motor last night. You helped us on ball control and that's about all."

"Yes, sir," muttered Stanton.

"Kutner, you had a chance to step in and play some basketball. You didn't do it. Hustle Stanton out of that forward's job if you feel like it. I want three men up on the boards, or four, even. Townsend, why is it you can't go up for rebounds on the attack? You handle the board fine on defense."

Craig sighed. If he resented the criticism, he did not show it. "Just never did," he said slowly. "I never played for anybody but Captain Wayne, and you know how he is. One guard is always in position to handle a fast break."

The coach nodded. That was certainly another Wayne trademark. But, as Denton recalled, the two guards divided this assignment almost equally. One fell back to cover as the other went in. But the Blue mentor, rather than pursue that subject now, shifted his attention to another player.

"We need more shooting, Tolar," he told the slim towhead. "If you can't deliver the baskets, I'll use Jamie. Sledge won't get loose like that again. No shooter scores in the thirties very often in this league. Ask Frank."

Hurst nodded. "You have to be hot and lucky both." He wanted to add that such a goalmaker had to be fed by his teammates from start to finish. No club had ever fed Frank as Craig, and the others had favored Sledge last night.

"Now let's work on these weaknesses," Denton said grimly. "We're just getting started. Remember that."

Two workouts produced little improvement. The Belmont coach wasn't a crepe-hanger, but he was willing to face facts. Probably his Blue outfit could repeat over Lafayette. Buster and Perry could raise their point production if the Green team clamped down on Crickett. Moss was sure to have a better night. Forrest Denton meant what he told sports writers. This club was hurt by Frank Hurst's absence. Any team needed a one-two scoring punch.

Craig Townsend read the newspaper quotations with mixed reactions. The Blues needed to develop another scorer, all right. Craig was disappointed, too, with Eddie's slow improvement. The lithe forward had taken one jump for the better but wasn't gaining.

But they would get by, mused Craig. Crickett could score twenty or more points anyhow. Townsend could handle the defensive post if he must. He sighed at the prospect. He disliked taking over the keyhole. No college coach would get excited about the defensive post work of a six-foot-three-inch player, but he could concede that much to the necessity of winning.

Craig drove Mary to school, a habit formed in this past week, as was meeting her after practice. It was easy to form such habits with Mary. Weekdays she was intent on her studies and her library duties. Having her as a steady girl friend didn't upset Craig's own full schedule. And Mary shed her academic personality on the weekends. Come

Friday night, and she was very much a normal girl—eager for the basketball game, the informal dances at the club, or a Sunday picnic if the weather permitted. She didn't expect much of him, and that was just what Craig wanted.

Now Celeste Petry would be different. She demanded attention. She said as much when Craig stopped outside the Science Building to talk with her.

"Going to take Lafayette tonight?"

He smiled. "That's up to Crickett and Eddie. They make the points."

Celeste's eyes gleamed. "They sure do. But you're not doing so bad yourself. Dad asked me about you yesterday. Said he never sees you except on Friday nights and then you're always off in some corner with Mary Tolar."

"Not always," he denied. "We dance some."

"She's not much of a dancer, is she?"

"No," Craig admitted. Mary enjoyed the informal hops, but she preferred to do more watching than participating.

"That's a shame," Celeste said lightly. "Takes a good dancer out of circulation." She sighed. "I'm not doing so well in that league either. Frank swears he won't get out on a dance floor until his ankle is completely well."

"You can't blame him for that."

"No," she conceded, "I suppose not, but it leaves me high and dry. Especially when Frank's team-mates consider me his personal property. I don't know where they get any such notion."

"I certainly have gotten it," Craig said. "You've been with him every time I've seen you," he added as she tossed her blonde head in protest.

"Sure. Nobody else ever asks me for a date. Nobody that I want to go with, anyhow."

Craig suppressed his smile. This role of a sad little rich girl, he was thinking, didn't fit Celeste Petry very well.

"Proclaim your independence," he said lightly. "Kick over the traces. Take the bull by the horns."

Celeste's eyes flashed. She had never found any young man so baffling. Was Craig Townsend blind to the advantages of having Herbert Petry's daughter as a girl friend? She doubted it. She was beginning to agree with her father—that this lean, rangy ex-airman was the coolest and smartest player Belmont had ever boasted.

"I could do that, I suppose," she said, a half-smile curving her lips. "I suppose I could come right out and ask for a date. I've never done it before, but there has to be a first time for everything."

"Sure," Craig said casually. "It wouldn't hurt

you to be turned down once. You can't win all the time."

"Would I be turned down—if I asked you?"

His lips twitched. He had foreseen that she was leading up to this, and he had already decided what to say. Craig's military service had taught him patience, even caution. He had realized for weeks that his aloofness bothered this spoiled blonde coed. It had been in the back of his mind all along to accept sometime the challenge of Celeste Petry's blue eyes. He needed her favor, for her father's influence if nothing else. But it would be a mistake to jump just because Celeste said "froggie." She was the type who would expect such a boy friend to keep right on hopping. There was much to be gained from a rich, influential patron; there was also a lot to be lost. Craig knew about a rumor that Mr. Petry was a bit disgusted with Frank Hurst.

"I'd have to turn you down," Craig said calmly. "I wouldn't want to." His grin spread wide. "You're a racehorse if I ever saw one. And I like the type, better than teacakes. But I got a girl friend, a nice one. She suits me pretty well. You would like for me to fill in while Frank is laid up. But you would jerk me back to the bench when he comes around to par again. That isn't for me, gal. I don't like warming the bench. I don't like standing in line."

He shook his head. "I stood in line for two years," he added. "For everything. Chow, uniforms, even to shoes. I had to take whatever the sergeant wanted to give me. No more of that line business for me."

Celeste's face crimsoned. "You're turning me down cold!" She couldn't believe it. Nothing like this had happened since she was thirteen years old.

"Not cold," denied Craig. "I'm just not volunteering to fill in for another guy. Get honest with yourself, chickadee. You aren't offering me a good deal, and I'm smart enough to know it. Give me credit for that."

"I will," snapped Celeste. "I certainly will. You're about the smartest person I know, Mr. Townsend. Maybe too smart for your own good."

He sighed as she went stomping off. Had he overdone it? There was no telling how much influence she had with her father or exactly what pull Herbert Petry had with Crownover. Craig shrugged away his worries. It must be considered a calculated risk. He had no intention of changing his way of handling his own affairs. He liked being his own playmaker. Let others take his signals and go into hurried motion. Those who didn't accept his system were welcome to get out of the picture—as Frank Hurst was easing himself out of the Belmont basketball line-up, and Perry Stanton and Jamie Brooks.

There were others to take their places. He could live without Celeste Petry's company. He liked Mary Tolar, and she wasn't the spoiled daughter of a millionaire. Like her brother, she appreciated Craig Townsend.

✿ ✿ ✿ ✿ ✿

Lafayette was out to stop Crickett Sledge. Craig realized that in the first minute of play. The capable Carl Bronson was sliding off to help guard the Blue pivot man. Craig called a time out with the green-clad visitors leading 3-0. Belmont had the antidote for this tight defense. In came Mark Kutner to replace Perry Stanton. Kutner broke in from the corner to hook the Blues' first field goal. Buster missed his first shot from outside the circle but got a quick second chance. Craig himself went up on the board to get the rebound and pass back to Buster. This time the towhead made good. His careful one-hander swished through, and Belmont led 4-3.

Craig talked to Crickett as the Blues took defensive positions. Play Perkins tight, he said. Return the favor—stop shooting under the basket. He and Buster would dog the out men, too. Let goals come few and hard. They could outrun these Lafayette opponents.

Crickett was no basket hog; happily the towering boy fed off to Eddie and Mark or back to Craig. After eight minutes of play Belmont led 15-10 and Sledge had not scored one field goal. He had sunk three efforts from the foul line as Bronson and Perkins overguarded him. Twice Eddie had broken through this staggered Green defense to drop crips in.

Jamie Brooks replaced Tolar. The substitution suited Craig; Buster was too reluctant to take outside shots. Jamie hit three baskets, and Kutner drove past his guard for another two points. Lafayette called time out for replacements and for a change in defensive strategy, too, guessed Craig, crouching on one knee before the Belmont bench. The scoreboard showed 23-14. Surely Lafayette's coach meant to loosen up his post defense.

But he didn't. He only replaced the two Green guards. The two proved to be even better shots than the starting pair. They were smaller, speedier boys. Craig and Jamie hustled hard but couldn't cover one-handers from the circle. Jamie especially couldn't. Buster had to come back in, and that weakened the Belmont attack.

The count became 31-26. Brooks gave Craig a breathing spell with two minutes left in the half.

"We're losing out on the backboard," Denton said worriedly. "Why can't Eddie work in better?"

Craig shook his head. He didn't understand that himself. He hated to admit it, but perhaps Moss just wasn't ready for full-time varsity play.

Denton guessed what his playmaker was thinking. The coach had formed the same conclusion. "I'm sending Perry in," Denton said. "Let's try three out."

He did not believe that Bronson would let Stanton go to double against Sledge. Belmont needed just one more offensive threat in order to occupy the stellar Green guard full time. Crickett could get away from Perkins for a few baskets, but he could not elude the combination of Lafayette's two best defensive men.

Denton sighed as he sat down again. He was right back where he had been at the start of the season—wishing that Townsend was more of a basket threat and less of a back court specialist.

That shift in scoring strategy earned Belmont two quick baskets. Then the Greens adapted themselves to this situation, too. They covered Perry closely and trailed only five points, 35-30, as the half ended.

❋ ❋ ❋ ❋ ❋

Only Craig Townsend's headwork was saving them, Coach Denton reflected as the score reached 48-41 halfway through the second period. The lean playmaker kept changing the Blue attack, capitalizing on Lafayette's teaming against Sledge. Eddie Moss turned in an offensive flurry before settling back into his ineffective groove. Jamie relieved Buster and sank two one-handers before the Green defense spread out to guard the circle.

Denton let Townsend call the turns, substituting as he realized the playmaker's changes in tactics. Paul Tipton took a turn for Moss, Kutner divided time with Perry, Jamie alternated with Buster. Each line-up change veered the Blue basket emphasis. Once Lafayette rallied to creep within two points, 57-55. But that surge wore out Perkins, and his replacement could not hold Crickett as well. Up went Sledge for three baskets in quick order. And that 63-55 margin allowed Belmont to begin ball control. Jamie moved to a forward post so that the Blues had four floor men in the line-up. Brooks, Tolar, and Stanton were good dribblers, Townsend a sure passer.

They forced the Green players out of a zone. Lafayette had to come after the ball. The visitors resorted to a full court press. Twice they grabbed possession in the back court, too, and made good both chances. But they fouled also, and Belmont converted most of these gratis tries. The game ended 70-59.

Coach Denton stood up with a sigh of relief. He was happy to have this game behind him.

There were six hurdles left now, home-and-home series with Calumet, Warmouth, and Hampton. All three were reckoned stronger than Lafayette. Glumly Denton talked over prospects with Cully Thomas. The assistant coach agreed that a double post was preferable to an inadequate three-in attack. Belmont could have a creditable double post offense when Frank Hurst returned to the line-up. Until then—well, Lady Luck had carried them this far, luck and a resourceful playmaker.

Where would the Blues be without Craig Townsend? Hopelessly mired in the second division, that was certain. A sudden whim struck Coach Denton as he sat brooding in his cubbyhole of an office. Suddenly he yielded to impulse and wrote a lengthy letter to Gilbert Wayne, the coaching genius he had never met. Wayne might reply; he might not.

Chapter Nine

Craig took the first opportunity to dance with Celeste. He and Mary had come late to the usual Petry reception. His eyes gleamed as he noticed the blonde girl's pique. So a young man had refused to jump through her hoop when she crooked her finger!

"You're a real doll tonight," he told Celeste. "Yellow is your color."

It was an attractive frock, all right. She had chosen it the previous week in Dallas. "I'm surprised you noticed it," Celeste said coldly. "You seem to be all tied up with brunettes and plain black dresses."

"Oh, no," denied Craig. "I just see how high a cliff is before I jump off, or how strong the limb is before I climb out on it."

A smile touched her lips. "I didn't think you were afraid of anything. Much less a skinny little girl."

"Are you skinny? I hadn't noticed it."

"Well, thanks. You are in high gear tonight, but then you ought to be. Dad thinks you're a cinch for all-conference. Said you might even be All-American if you could shoot baskets."

"I can shoot baskets," Craig said lightly. "Just never got around to it. I stay pretty busy on the court, if you haven't noticed it."

"You do," nodded Celeste. The music stopped; she gestured to the open doorway. "It's a pretty night outside. Let's get some air, or are you afraid to risk it?"

He smiled at her taunt. "Oh, I'm not really afraid. For all I know your bark might be worse than your bite."

She tossed her blonde head. "Don't count on that. It's possible you can be wrong about some things."

She shivered a little outside but refused to return immediately. "I don't like the way you're treating me," she said tersely. "You like things laid on the line, don't you?"

"I sure do. I'm no hand for double talk."

"You don't want to play second fiddle to Frank, do you?"

Craig smiled. "On a basketball court, yes. Let him be the fair-haired boy for another year. I helped him set a new scoring record. Then I helped

Sledge break it. As soon as Frank's ready, I'll help him put Crickett's mark in the shade. His name will go into the record books and maybe stay there a long while. That doesn't bother me a bit. That's the playmaker's job, to make the guys up front look good. I work at that job. It's my trade for the next eight or ten years. Hurst, Sledge—it doesn't matter to me who holds the records."

He grinned. "But off the court—in the moonlight —and a pretty girl near by, I don't go for any second-fiddle stuff. I'm going to direct the band, or I won't put in my nickel."

She couldn't help smiling. "You're a character, Craig. You have everything figured out, don't you?"

"Just about."

"You shy off from deals that don't make sense?"

"I sure do."

"For instance," she said slowly, "you wouldn't throw jealous tantrums every time your girl friend paid attention to someone else?"

"I don't think so. I never could afford jealousy."

"Frank is terribly jealous of me. Did you know that?"

"I'm not surprised."

"And I'm not near ready to get dead serious about him." Celeste tossed her head. "I have some rather definite plans for the next few years myself. You're not the only person who can chart his own course."

"I'm sure not." He hesitated. "It should be easier for you, too. I have to meet the cost as I go along. I can't be sure about a university yet. I have my eye on Crownover. But if they don't offer me a scholarship—and some other school does—"

Craig shrugged his shoulders. "Oh, I'll get another offer, all right. Some Eastern college will make me a deal on Gilbert Wayne's say-so. His word is basketball gospel back there. In the Midwest, too. Around here," he sighed, "I'm not the flashy type, chick. I don't show up so good on paper. I'm not tree-top tall, and I'm not a showboat. I don't know whether I'll get a tumble from Crownover or not. I'm afraid I won't."

"You would if Dad said so," Celeste said briskly. "Already he has lined Frank up, or almost."

"I know that. I'm sure Crownover will take one player out of respect for your father. They can hardly do anything else. But your father helped raise Frank. And—" he smiled and waved his hands— "your father must consider Frank a prospective son-in-law."

"My father has nothing to do with that," snapped Celeste. "And I'm not sure Dad is too sold on Frank's basketball future."

"What do you mean?"

"This season has sort of opened his eyes. Frank pumps in some baskets and that's all. Dad admires your playmaking. You should cultivate him more. He says you're hard to know."

Craig hid his pleased smile. He had wanted Herbert Petry to notice and appreciate the fact that at least one ambitious Belmont cager did not presume on a ready generosity. "All I have to offer Crownover is my basketball playing," he said. "I hope they take notice of it. I'd appreciate your father or anyone else calling it to their attention. But if they look me over, and don't want me, then I don't want them."

"We'd better go inside," said Celeste. "I'm chilly."

But she stopped him at the door. "Effective next week," she said, "I'm no longer going steady with Frank. I'm not telling him to go peddle his papers or anything like that. There's no point in it. But little Celeste will be available. Will you be at all interested, Mr. Townsend?"

"Sure," smiled Craig. "All I ask is a fair shake."

He surrendered her to Perry Stanton and watched as she whirled over the floor with Frank's closest friend. Probably Hurst had sent Perry to find Celeste and get her away from Craig. The good-looking dark-haired youth didn't conceal his jealousy very well. He stood across the dance floor now, scowling a little. Plainly he did not like the way things were going.

And Craig Townsend did. So Herbert Petry was wondering why Belmont's new cage star didn't wangle his help toward a Crownover scholarship! Craig had hoped for just that reaction. He had learned quite a bit about human nature during his military service. The wise enlisted man never openly proposed that an officer do anything. He maneuvered the officer into having the idea himself. When that was done, the officer put the idea into immediate and enthusiastic effect. The thing to do was to let Herbert Petry decide on his own that his alma mater could make good use of Craig's playmaking ability. It wouldn't hurt, of course, for Celeste to make a suggestion to the rich man. And she would, Craig was sure of that. His ideas about handling her were coming along. He had not wanted to be the direct cause of her breakup with Frank Hurst. He didn't want the scoring ace's hostility. They had to work more closely together the rest of this season. A goal hawk needed a playmaker, but then the floor general also required the services of a crack shot. Eddie Moss was not developing as Craig had hoped.

This way, mused Craig, he was not the "nigger in the woodpile." Not at all. He hadn't even asked

Celeste for a date yet; Frank couldn't claim that a teammate had run under him.

*   *   *   *   *

Frank still favored his ankle, but he insisted that he was ready for full practice and part-time play, at least. "You'll need me to beat Calumet," he insisted to Coach Denton.

The mentor couldn't deny that. The Cougars were rated slightly stronger than Winston or Lafayette. Dr. Ralph Hannah reluctantly agreed to let Frank suit out. "It won't do him any good," said the physician, "but if he will take it easy—and isn't left in too long—it shouldn't hurt him."

Craig welcomed Hurst's availability for part-time duty. "Crickett needs to be spelled. Frank can pick up the slack while Barley is in there."

Coach Denton nodded. That was his idea exactly. He would convert the Blue attack to a two-three pattern, Sledge and Moss in, then Hurst and Barley. Perry Stanton would play most of the time at forward. Townsend must go the full forty minutes. Tolar and Jamie would alternate at the other guard spot, with the latter's play coinciding with Frank's turn at forward. There was no use of the coach's wondering why Hurst scored more with Jamie and

Perry on the floor. If there was any sort of personality clash involved, neither Frank nor Craig showed it. But the coach had to face facts at this stage of the season. There wasn't time for experiments in psychology.

The first game with the Cougars was in the Belmont gym, for which Denton was grateful. Hurst could be used more in the second game. And Denton figured Hurst must account for any difference between the two quintets.

The Cougars started a fivesome of four speedsters and one big hulking player near Crickett's height and thirty pounds heavier. Denton guessed their defensive pattern before the tip-off. Every report about Calumet had described Troy Peterson as a rough goal defender. The Cougar center confirmed those stories immediately. He threw his weight as he and Sledge went up together for a rebound. It wasn't a foul; both players were after the ball. But certainly Peterson grabbed the chance to shake up Belmont's beanpole. He passed off to a teammate, and Calumet revealed its fast-moving, free-shooting attack.

They meant to outrun the Blues. Denton's starting line-up was about his best combination against speed—Moss and Perry at forwards, Crickett in the slot, Craig and Buster at the two guard positions.

He must spell them, mused Denton, even Craig. Otherwise they'd be run dizzy and throw away scoring opportunities. It wasn't easy for a quintet to shift from breakneck defense to careful deliberate attack. It took a playmaker of exceptional leadership to turn the trick.

Craig Townsend could. He kept his teammates calm on the attack, even Sledge. Crickett got the ball in the post again and again. But Peterson pressed him hard, and the lanky Blue ace got off only two shots in the first five minutes. Both were good, and Eddie Moss slipped past his defender to record a field goal. Craig converted a free throw, and Perry two out of three gratis chances, accounting for Belmont's 9-7 lead at the first full time out.

"You're doing fine," Denton told his perspiring charges. "Keep making your chances count and don't worry about their running shots from the outside. You can't stop that kind of shots and don't worry about them. They're hitting 40 per cent now; I don't believe they can keep it up. Anybody winded?"

"I'm close to it," confessed Stanton, "but I'll make it a while longer."

Craig Townsend got up from the floor. "They're all over Sledge in the post. That guard, Jackson, helps out some. If Frank spelled Perry, they'd watch him close. They'd have to, even if he took it easy."

Denton nodded. The left-handed forward was that much respected as a threat. Calumet would widen its cover around the slot to include Hurst. But would Frank be careful of that ankle? Wouldn't he insist upon driving himself hard?

"I'll talk to him," decided the coach. "We may try it." The threat of Frank Hurst could not be overlooked even if he did not stage his usual twisting shots.

Denton motioned Hurst to sit by him. "Could you take it slow a few minutes? Do more faking than shooting? Feed Ed Barley and Crickett?"

"I can handle it," promised the eager veteran. "I may limp around some, but I'm good for a few baskets."

"You'll loosen 'em up just being on the floor. Don't put too much on that ankle."

Frank stripped off his sweat togs and hurried to the scorer's table. A cheer went up as Belmont rooters saw him crouched, waiting to go in at the first time out. Coach Denton covered his smile with the palm of his hand. Most of the Blues' supporters believed the team went as Frank went. If he was hot, Belmont won. If he had a bad night, the Blues lost.

That had been true the previous year, but not

this year. Craig Townsend had transformed this Blue squad. Hurst could help mightily, yes—if he would play ball control, feed off to Crickett or Eddie, and shoot only when good openings came. But why expect him to do that? He had never played ball control. He had carried the brunt of his team's scoring efforts since his sophomore year in high school.

Craig flipped to Buster. Tolar threw in to Eddie. The slender forward juggled the pass and had the ball knocked out of his clutching fingers. Crickett slapped the sphere over to Craig. This tall center was working to learn ball control. He no longer lost his head when smothered by a tight defense. Craig threw to Buster. Tolar passed to Hurst. Up went the forward for his favorite shot. The ball spun around the rim, then fell through.

How he could make those shots—with little or no arch, no sort of spin—wasn't easy to explain. But the shot was in. The Blues led 11-7. And, at the first chance, Coach Denton rushed Jamie Brooks in at guard. Why expect Hurst to change his ways overnight? The forward meant to seize every opportunity to shoot. He would make chances if they didn't develop normally. That was the only basketball Hurst knew.

He hit three times in as many minutes. Not in

succession, however. Four times his flat efforts bounced crazily off the hoop and into Cougar hands. Another off-balance shot fell short and out of bounds. Calumet converted two of those five opportunities into baskets. The score stood 16-11 when Perry and Buster returned to action, sending Frank and Jamie to the bench.

"Good work," Denton told his black-haired star. "I don't want you overdoing it."

The Blue coach realized Frank's weaknesses as well as any other cage authority. But Denton's evaluation made sense, too. Frank had staged a one-man offensive flurry. He hadn't helped work the ball in for a sure shot once. But Belmont had gained two points in the southpaw's brief playing time. There was no use in going wild about a pointmaker, true. Hurst lacked a lot of deserving his reputation. But neither was there any use in selling him short. He was a threat to score any time he got the ball.

What would he do the rest of the season? Use Frank for brief flurries, keep him benched the rest of the time? Maybe, mused Denton, that ankle injury had established Frank's proper place in the Belmont line-up. For Belmont clung to a four-point advantage until the last four minutes of the half. Then Denton returned Hurst to the court for the rest of the period. He tallied three baskets and a free try while the visitors registered four points. The score was 29-22 at intermission.

Craig slumped to the dressing-room floor, tired and willing to admit it. He had gone the whole twenty minutes, and the Cougar forwards had run him ragged.

"I'll spell you off next half," promised Denton.

"You'll have to," nodded the lean guard. "They're jack rabbits. And you must watch every one of them."

That was quite true. Calumet had no scoring principal. Their tall boy was their weakest player on attack. Defense against these Cougars called for speed and endurance. Denton knew what to do this second half. Substitute Frank, Barley, and Jamie together, replacing Eddie, Crickett, and Craig. Let his Blue cagers revert to their attack of the previous year. It wasn't a bad offense. Calumet's smaller guards couldn't check it. The visitors would have to make substitutions, too, realign their defense. The tight zone which smothered Sledge would not handcuff Lefty Hurst.

The score was 37-31 when Denton sent in replacements. For four hectic minutes Frank banged away at the basket while his teammates scampered desperately to recover his missed shots. It was an abrupt change in strategy. The fans roared approval. This type of game was more exciting, all right. It certainly wasn't as sound. When Hurst left the court, the gymnasium cheered him for his nine points in four minutes. He was leading Belmont's pointmakers with 14. In that same time Calumet had narrowed the margin to 47-42. Frank's splurge had actually cost a point. But Coach Denton was satisfied. He had rested Craig, Crickett, and Tolar. That was the real worth of Hurst's one-man show. It wasn't to be discounted.

For that respite, and another three-minute one, enabled Townsend, Sledge, and Buster to finish strong. They choked off a desperate Calumet rally in the closing minutes. The game ended 63-56.

Denton's lips twitched as he followed his charges to the dressing room. The individual points were being recited over the loudspeaker.

". . . For Belmont, Frank Hurst was high-point man with 20 points. Crickett Sledge had 15, Perry Stanton nine . . ."

High-point man despite only 15 minutes of playing time! Denton could imagine the morning newspaper account. "Although held to a substitute's role by an injured ankle, veteran Frank Hurst led Belmont to a 63-56 win over Calumet Tuesday night."

152

It would go something like that anyhow; newspaper stories always did.

❊   ❊   ❊   ❊   ❊

Frank was obviously happy about being the center of attention in the dressing room. He sat smiling
on a bench while the team doctor unwrapped gauze
and adhesive tape from his ankle.

"Boy, you saved our hides," praised Perry. "You
didn't overdo it, did you?"

"It hurts," admitted Hurst of his ankle. The
physician studied the swollen ankle critically.

"There's more swelling," he declared, "but not
too much. You can play some Friday, if you'll stay
down until then."

"I'll do it," promised Frank.

The doctor rebandaged the ankle. Frank tested
his weight on it gingerly. "I'll make it," grinned
the forward. "Count me out of social life for a few
days, but I'll play some Friday night. And full
time against Warmouth."

Coach Denton kept his thoughts to himself as he
left the dressing room. He doubted that Hurst
would be used full time again this season. The coach
certainly meant to repeat the same strategy against
the Cougars. It could be truthfully said, reflected

Denton, that he was planning to use the two-platoon system. He doubted if that strategy would win the championship, but he was convinced it was the best possible use of his players. Here with only five conference games left, Belmont was no stronger on the boards than when the season opened.

The coach remembered his topcoat, turned back to get it, and met Craig Townsend.

"Got a heavy date?" Denton asked pleasantly. He was no longer worried about the "lone wolf" ways of the Blue playmaker. From all reports Craig was gaining social popularity.

"I have hopes," Craig said. "You never can tell. I might be too late."

"Dodge the heavy traffic. There are too many cute girls here to be fighting over a few."

Craig nodded. He had been doing that for almost a month. Mary Tolar kept carefully out of the full social whirl. She had discouraged so many fellow students that Craig had not been bothered with competition. But he was thinking about Celeste Petry tonight. Frank had orders to go directly to bed. Besides, Celeste had declared herself back in circulation. A telephone call might find her available.

Coach Denton hesitated. Should he say anything to Craig about how he intended to use Frank in the future? The coach felt that he should. He couldn't remember another junior-college player shouldering as much responsibility as this lean guard. The term "one-man team" usually referred to its leading scorer. But that was not true of the Belmont Blues. It was built around a player with a marked aversion for pointmaking.

"Frank helped us tonight," Denton said cautiously. How did Hurst and Craig actually feel about each other? The coach had observed no resentment in either. There seemed to be nothing personal about their inability to work together.

"He surely did," Craig said readily. He sighed. "He can hit that bucket, Coach. Sometimes I get a little disgusted with him. I oughtn't say that, but I do. When he swings out, when he hits a streak, it's like he's the only player on the court. He just takes over for two or three minutes."

Denton's eyes gleamed in approval. He should have known Townsend would quickly realize Frank's value as a spot player.

"If we can use him for his streaks from now on— run him in and out—will it work?" asked the coach.

"It should," Craig said promptly. "If you can keep him satisfied that way."

Coach Denton sighed. There was the rub. How could he reconcile Frank to a substitute's role? He considered a direct approach to his veteran forward, then changed his mind. Frank's weakened ankle settled the problem for the time being. The unpleasant task could be put off for a week at least.

❊   ❊   ❊   ❊   ❊

Celeste was at home and not very happy about it. But she declined to accept a date at this late hour.

"I'm in circulation, all right, and there isn't a line outside. But I won't be picked up as a last resort. What's the trouble? Mary busy?"

"I don't know," Craig said truthfully. "I haven't called her."

"That's something. It seemed to me I was second choice. Or even fourth or fifth."

"No, it has just taken me this long to get up my nerve."

Celeste laughed. "I've noticed how you like to stay in the background. Father tells me you played good basketball again. He's worried about how he can get Crownover's coaches to realize your real value to the team. He says he hasn't any clippings to send them."

"No. I need a publicity man."

"Take lessons from Frank."

"Why not let him keep his headlines and let me have his girl?"

"I'm not his girl."

"His ex-girl, then."

"I might agree to that," Celeste said calmly. "The place is open. You can try out Friday night if you're interested."

Craig hesitated. He was sure that Mary was counting on him for the usual club dance. But Craig had not committed himself.

"I'd have to be late. We're playing at Calumet."

"Of course. I'll be there. You can drive my car home."

"I'm not sure I would know how to drive such a late model. I've never driven one like it."

"It practically drives itself. And I'm a willing back-seat driver."

"Then I'll risk it."

Now, he mused, how to handle Mary? He did not know how she felt about him. Most of their contacts were casual. She studied at the library until after basketball practice; Craig and Buster went by for her. They let Buster out at home if other plans arose; Craig visited a while in the Tolar home otherwise. He sighed. He liked the Tolars. But the school year was moving along. Five more games and the cage season would be over. Celeste was his best chance to develop the one personal contact which would move Crownover to action.

That contact, of course, was Mr. Herbert Petry. Craig was more interested in the father than the daughter. Celeste was attractive, very, an appealing girl. But Mr. Petry's influence with Crownover coaches was more important.

The chance to let Mary down gently came Thursday night. Craig, Buster, Crickett, and the darkhaired girl sat around the big kitchen table in the Tolar home and consumed a homemade angel food cake.

Motherly Mrs. Tolar scoffed at literal observance of training rules. "Good food," she said, "is always good for you, till you get too fat. And you boys are skinny as fence rails."

The team would travel by bus to the Calumet gymnasium. Coach Denton insisted on that. The players could return any way they chose, but they must go over together.

"That puts a crimp in my plans," complained Buster. He grinned. "I hadn't asked, Craig, but I've counted on using your back seat coming home. Jean Kelly is the lucky girl."

Craig frowned. He was driving Celeste's car back.

158

"You can have my car," he offered. "Mary can drive it over."

She shook her head. "No. Something might happen."

"It's good for another thirty miles," claimed the owner. "I've another way back, but that doesn't matter. You can bring the car to school Saturday."

Buster shook his head. "If you're not coming back with us, we can't just borrow the car for the trip."

"Indeed you cannot," ruled Mrs. Tolar. "There's a special bus making the trip. You and Miss Jeannie girl can just ride it."

"And it will be eleven o'clock before we get back," said Buster. "Oh, well, she'll just have to like it."

Obviously Craig's announcement of other plans for Friday night cast a damper over the group. He tried to ease the situation later, talking to Mary on the front porch.

"Frank is still favoring his ankle," he explained. "Celeste said there was no point of her father putting on the dance if his own daughter didn't have a date."

"And you volunteered," guessed Mary. "I'm not surprised, Craig. Disappointed, yes, but not crushed. Don't suffer any qualms of conscience."

His jaw tightened. He wasn't sure he appreciated her attitude. "You're not too puzzling a young man, Craig," Mary said quietly. "I'm older than Buster or Crickett, or even Celeste Petry. The necessity of earning money slowed down my school progress, too. I know what it is to wait and watch for opportunities."

"What do you mean?"

"Just that," she answered. "You're the determined sort. You're thinking about the future. Bucking for OCS—isn't that what they say in the Army? You'll go a long way, Craig."

His lean face showed his resentment. "Aren't you jumping to conclusions? I'm just taking Celeste to one dance."

Mary shook her head. "No, Craig. Celeste may think that now; so might Frank. But that isn't how I'm betting." She held out her hand. "Good luck, Craig. I don't blame you a bit. You've had a hard go of it. You would be a fool not to jump at a chance to make things easier. And you're no fool. You're as shrewd as they come."

"Thank you," Craig said tersely.

"To my way of thinking," continued this surprising girl, "you're going about things the wrong way. You're calling all the shots yourself. You think other people are going to fit into your pattern and stay put. They won't, Craig. But you'll have to learn for yourself. You can manipulate people pretty well. You have the basketball team toeing your line, except for Frank. He won't do it, Craig. He'll kick over the traces."

"I didn't realize you were such a basketball expert," he snapped.

"I know my brother and Crickett and Ed Barley," Mary said quietly. "You've taught them some tricks, and they'll jump through your hoop any time you say. And I think I know you, too, Craig. I'm finding out the things that puzzled me at first." Her lips twitched, and she shook her dark head. "I wish things weren't so obvious. So long, Craig. Good luck. I mean it."

He forced a smile. "What is this exactly? Am I getting my walking papers?"

"Sort of." Her eyes fell, then came up, and met his squarely. "I've done my trick. You don't need me in the act any more. I haven't a rich father who helps deserving basketball players."

She turned. The door closed behind her immediately. Craig Townsend looked after her a moment, then walked to his car. She was a shrewd little cookie, he mused. Nobody could accuse Mary Tolar of not knowing the score. Much more likable than Celeste, too. Even prettier in her subdued

161

sort of way. But she had called the deal right. Craig had to see to a lot of things before he could take any girl seriously. Maybe in two more years, when he was finishing his college play, when professional scouts were bidding for his signature, when he had an insurance or bond company connection and could cash in on his contacts with wealthy, influential people. . . .

He looked back at the Tolar house and sighed. Theirs was a happy life. They put warmth and affection first, instead of money and influence. Craig might have been like that himself, if things had been different. But they were not. He started his car and drove off. There was nothing to be unhappy about, he told himself. He had felt this loneliness before. He had lived with it for four years. He had learned how to beat it down.

*　*　*　*　*

Frank insisted his ankle was as good as new, but Coach Denton refused to revise his plans. Stanton and Moss at forwards, Sledge at center, Townsend and Tolar at guards.

"We'll run off their edge," Denton told Frank, "then send you in."

Hurst unhappily joined the row of blue-clad substitutes. He would start the next game anyhow, he assured himself. Even if he still favored his ankle, he was the most dangerous basketmaker in the conference. It wouldn't take him long to prove that again. Just one nod of Coach Denton's head and Belmont would be widening its margin, not slowing down to a deliberate attack every time the Blues got possession.

The score reached 9-7. Then Crickett relaxed his vigilance on burly Joe Peterson, and the Cougar center went up on the rim to tie the score. Sledge fouled, too; Peterson calmly sank the free try. The Calumet gymnasium rocked with applause. The speedy Cougars were out in front 10-9.

Denton gestured to Tolar to call time out. Frank hurriedly pulled off his sweat suit. So did Jamie Brooks. Out came Moss and Tolar.

"Stay ready," the coach told Buster. "You'll be going right back in."

Denton meant to spell Craig, too. If Frank was his usual self, then the Blue team would get by a few minutes on his single-handed brilliance. The determined Hurst cut loose immediately. Calumet couldn't adjust its defense so quickly. Three players must be replaced and going at top efficiency before the Cougars could subdue this whirling, leaping southpaw. Frank swished four fallaway shots through the net. He scored two more points from the foul line. Sledge batted in a rebound. Perry and Jamie were each fouled as they fought to feed Frank.

Calumet scored, too—eight points. But Belmont led 21-18 when Lefty Hurst came off the floor with disgust written all over his dark features. He could not understand Denton's strategy. What was wrong with ten points in five minutes!

But Coach Denton knew what he was about. Craig knew what to do, too. The Blues did not resume their deliberate offense immediately. The Cougar defense was set up now for plays into the keyhole. Three times Crickett went up for crips before Calumet revised its backboard pattern, assigning both guards to float over when the tall center had the ball. Jamie hit twice from the outside against this tight zone defense. Coach Denton clucked in satisfaction as the score reached 33-24. His glance went to the impatient Hurst. How things could change in a year's time, mused Denton. A year ago Frank had been getting more credit than he deserved. Now it was the other way around. The average fan could not realize the value of such a substitute.

Twice in the last half Frank took the court for reckless, dizzy outbursts. The Blue quintet matched his tempo. Denton carefully kept in the line-up the boys who would—Mark Kutner at center, Perry, Jamie, and Buster. Then out came all but Stanton and Tolar, and the Belmont line-up changed into a cool, methodical court machine which made few mistakes and allowed few baskets.

The final score was 66-53. Overjoyed Belmont students poured out onto the court and paraded two new heroes on their shoulders. It had taken most of the season, but now both fans and sports writers realized who made this unbeaten Blue team click. A substitute forward had scored 19 points, true, but where would Belmont be without Craig Townsend? Not challenging Hampton and Warmouth for the championship, that was certain.

✽ ✽ ✽ ✽ ✽

At the dance later that night Herbert Petry echoed this enthusiasm for the Blues' playmaker.

"You're so danged willing to stay in the background," complained the millionaire patron of Belmont Junior College. "A person has to look twice to be sure you're on the court, much less realize how this team is built around you. You're a hard man to sell, Townsend. I talked to Bart Millican, the Crownover coach, last night. He had heard some nice things about you, all right. But he asked in the next breath how Frank was doing."

Craig's eyes gleamed. Herbert Petry was promoting him with Crownover's coaching staff without being asked!

"I appreciate that, Mr. Petry. That was the big reason why I chose Belmont. I knew that Crownover took Belmont stars regularly. Gil Wayne told me that. I didn't know that you were the man responsible, not until I came here."

"Oh, yes," said Mr. Petry. "Bart will always take one player on my say-so. Well, not every time, but mostly. Crownover is limited to ten new scholarships a year." The rich man sighed. "I've never yet talked Bart into taking two Belmont players, though. And Frank has the inside track. Bart looked him over a couple of times last year."

"Well," Craig said carefully, "all I can do is keep working, and hoping."

He went back to the dance floor. Time was running short. He had just two weeks to insure the full endorsement of both father and daughter. If Crownover would take only one graduate of this Belmont team, then Frank Hurst had better scout around for another college. Craig Townsend meant to be first choice.

Chapter Ten

Coach Denton took his squad to watch the second Warmouth-Hampton game. The Warmouth Warriors were unbeaten, too, having downed the Hampton Hornets 72-71. Hampton had no other losses. A Hornet win in this second clash would help the Blues' chances no little. And that was just what happened. Hampton won 75-70, leaving Belmont the only unbeaten team in the conference.

But could the Blues beat either the Hornets or the Warriors? Denton prepared careful notes on both future opponents. He suspected that Warmouth would be the tougher. The Warrior center, Felix McCabe, was the best in the conference. He stood six-eight and handled himself smoothly. Sledge was almost sure to foul out if assigned to guard such a threat full time.

Hampton's tallest player stood only six-six. Crickett's height advantage should net the Blues several points in each game. But the two Hornet forwards were six-five and six-four. A guard was six-five, too. Crickett would be a lone threat on the boards against such a combination. And how could Sledge defend the Belmont basket against four tall opponents?

The coach saw only one solution. Craig and Crickett must team together on defense. He sketched some crude diagrams. Sledge was too slow for anything but a zone, and personal fouls entered into the picture. Could Townsend let the first Hampton player go, take the second, or shift to meet any break by another tall Hornet? Craig nodded. He would try it. The lean playmaker agreed with Coach Denton. Their defense would tell the story against Hampton.

Frank spoke out against his substitute's role. His ankle was almost as good as new, he claimed. He was sure he could go all the way with it taped tightly.

Denton explained the strategy for the next series, or at least the first game. The Blue team would depend on Frank's flurries for leads and concentrate on defense the rest of the time.

"I don't want you wearing yourself out against a taller man," Coach Denton explained reassuringly. "We're hoping your nineteen or twenty points will be the difference."

"I hope so," Frank said glumly. He looked away. "This team doesn't depend on me much any more," he said almost bitterly. "I never thought I'd be benched in my last season."

"You aren't benched exactly," Denton pointed out. "You're still the team's high-point man."

"Sure," admitted Frank. "But do you think I'll still get a Crownover bid—sitting on the bench?"

The coach frowned. "I thought you had that sewed up. Didn't Mr. Petry arrange that last winter?"

"Not finally. They would have taken me last spring all right, but I wanted to finish up here. So they said they'd wait and see."

"Surely Mr. Petry will keep pressure on them?" Then the coach remembered a snatch of talk he had overheard. "Or will he?"

"I'm not sure," Frank said unhappily. He gestured helplessly with both hands. "Townsend has moved in on me there, too."

Denton sighed. He could not deny that Craig had developed into Belmont's floor leader. The Blues' emphasis was on new players except for Frank's scoring outbursts. Crickett, Eddie, and Buster had relegated Perry and Jamie to secondary roles. But the Blue coach offered no excuses. The results justified his line-up changes. Belmont was unbeaten with only four games left.

"Townsend is quite a ball player, Frank," Denton said gently. "He's the best playmaker in the conference and one of the top defensive hands. If Crickett had to carry his full load in the keyhole—well, he just couldn't."

"Oh, sure," Frank Hurst said quickly. "I'm not trying to take a thing away from Townsend. The guy's a regular machine. Moss says he's rough on the boards, too. You could use him in my place if you had to."

"Not on the boards. He can't or he won't." Denton slapped Frank's shoulder. "Don't give up on that Crownover bid, son. You'll get plenty of chances in these next two weeks. You're still the best basket hawk in this part of the country."

"I'm ready any time."

The conversation appeared to ease Frank's resentments. The veteran forward hoarsely voiced enthusiasm to the Belmont starters. "You characters gotta hold 'em. Townsend, boy, we're depending on you."

There was nothing wrong with Frank's attitude, reflected Denton. The veteran had given his best all season. If he had done little but shoot baskets, that was because he had developed no other ability.

Nearly all the Belmont student body had followed the team to Hampton. The gymnasium was jammed as a result. And the din was terrific even before the first shot was attempted. Bob Greer, one of Hampton's rangy forwards, took a backward lob from his post man and drove for the basket. A blue-clad figure cut around him, snaked the ball out of his hands. Buster scooped up the deflected ball and Belmont moved to attack.

Coach Denton's eyes gleamed. The Blue defense had worked like a charm. Craig had darted off from one Hornet to steal the ball from another. The two-on-one defense wasn't new to this conference. But how about the one-on-two? Who had ever heard of such a defense?

Crickett's reach must pay off; the Blue offense was geared to it. Perry, Buster, and Eddie took their turns feinting to go up for shots. Then came what they were waiting for. Sledge slid away from his opponent, and Eddie arched the ball toward the hoop. Crickett lifted it into the netting with his fingertips. Belmont had drawn first blood!

But Greer, Mutt Camp, Bruno Johnson, and Paul Hardy moved in on Craig, Eddie, and Sledge. Johnson pitched back to Hardy. Another time Craig guessed the Hornet intent. He slapped the ball hard. Perry Stanton took it downcourt on a fast dribble. He bounced off to Buster and the tow-headed guard sank an easy crip.

"By golly," chortled Frank, "we're going to do it, Coach! That Townsend knows their plays better than they do."

"He's a born playmaker," said Denton. "Remember that when you get in there. Let Craig call the turn. If he leads you, go in and up. If he doesn't, pass the ball on."

Frank's head dropped. He looked up shortly, his lips tight. "I don't expect anybody to believe it," he said slowly, "but I *have* tried to work with Townsend."

"Tried your best?"

"Not all the time, I'll admit, but some. More than he's tried to work with me." The dark-haired player sighed. "But that's crying over spilled milk. Townsend does a good job of running the team. He got us this far. I know that better than anybody else."

Coach Denton nodded. The blue-jerseyed team capitalized on another Hampton mistake. Eddie made this basket, and Belmont led 6-0. But Denton knew this one-sided business would not last. The Hornet attack was the most versatile he had seen all year. Greer and Hardy hit field goals, and Camp sank a free try. Then Eddie put the Blues ahead 8-5. He drove through two Hornet defenders to sink his hook shot. It was smart, hard driving. Give us that kind of board play, mused Coach Denton, and we'll take everybody in this league.

Baskets by Greer and Hardy gave Hampton a 9-8 lead with seven minutes gone. Denton sent in Hurst and Jamie. The Blues changed tactics immediately. The careful deliberate game turned into a wild scramble. Frank's fallaway shots were missing, and the cool Hornet quintet exploited the rebounds. Denton let the score reach 19-18 before returning his starting line-up to the game.

"I couldn't hit, Coach," groaned Frank.

Denton nodded. His gamble had failed. But Craig and Eddie had grabbed a few minutes of rest. Promptly Townsend slowed down the Belmont attack. The ball went from player to player until Eddie found an opening. The slim forward pulled back as he brushed against the tight Hampton zone. He simply wasn't the offensive spark Belmont needed.

But the Blues held even. Crickett rolled three field goals into the hoop. He converted two out of three chances from the foul line. Spared the grueling defensive chore under his own goal, Sledge was battling for baskets with more determination than he had showed all season. Perry Stanton was turning in a fine game, too. He lacked the height to stop Hampton's jump shooters, but he harried them relentlessly, forcing hurried shots. The Hornets led 26-20 with six minutes to go. Denton sent Hurst in for Eddie Moss but kept Jamie out of action. Craig was doing too much on defense.

Townsend bounced the ball in to Hurst; up went the veteran, twisting backward. His shot caromed off the board and into the netting. The referee ruled that Frank had been fouled in the act of shooting. He sank the free try, too. Then he took the Hornet team by surprise with a bold swipe at the ball. He knocked it downcourt and outran a Hampton opponent. Another Hornet rushed in to help cover the Belmont ace. Up twisted Hurst with both opponents almost hanging on his neck. Somehow he got the ball away. It rolled around the hoop for an awful second and then fell through. The referee's whistle announced another penalty against Hampton for overguarding. His dark features grim, Frank added this point while the Blue supporters went wild. The score was tied at 26-26! In just 45 furious seconds this fiery Blue forward had evened the score.

Nor was he through. Perry hurtled forward and batted a Hornet pass to Buster. Tolar fed the ball to Craig. Townsend did not hesitate. He whipped the ball downcourt to Hurst. The black-haired veteran ignored Sledge. Up went Hurst himself into a tangle of arms. The ball plopped heavily into the netting.

The rattled Hampton quintet called time out, for which Denton was grateful. These furious forays took all of Frank's strength. He was panting now, spent. The Belmont coach hesitated, then gestured to Eddie. Out came Hurst with the Blue supporters roaring in dismay. But Frank showed neither surprise nor resentment. He was completely spent and realized it.

"That's just what the doctor ordered, son," Denton told Hurst. "Give us another spree, and we'll wrap up this game."

"You'll get it," promised Frank.

Hampton started upcourt with the ball, and Belmont's ruse took even Coach Denton by surprise. Suddenly the Blues put on a full court press. The gamble worked. Buster intercepted a hurried pass, and Eddie dropped in the ball. Craig broke up the next Hornet play before it was launched, leaving his keyhole post as he outguessed the Hampton guards. The lean playmaker refused to dribble in. He handed off to Perry, who banked in a sharply angled shot. Belmont led 36-32.

Then back to a tight Blue defense. Hampton's Greer made the only other basket before the half ended.

*　*　*　*　*

Coach Denton had no intention of changing line-up or strategy. This, he was sure, was his wisest use of material. It might not make good sense to divide his offensive and defensive standouts, but it worked. Given a four-point lead, Craig, Buster, Crickett, Perry, and Eddie battled Hampton grimly for nine full minutes. The score stood 42-40 then, with Hampton leading.

That score, however, did not represent the whole picture. Paul Hardy of Hampton had four fouls and went to the bench. Greer, Camp, and Johnson had played the entire time without relief. The Hornet line-up as play resumed included two sub-stitutes, and Hampton lacked depth. Denton sent in Hurst, Barley, and Jamie at the next opportunity.

Frank rolled in two of his fallaway shots, but the Hornets didn't react as expected. They took the 46-40 score calmly enough, moving deliberately to clear Greer or Johnson under the basket. Craig Townsend was missed sorely on defense. Sledge had to battle the board single-handed and fouled twice in as many minutes. Then Hampton revealed another antidote for Hurst's basket magic. Camp dogged the Blue forward all over the court, refusing to let Frank get set at the top of the circle.

And Hampton pulled closer. The score reached 48-46. Frank pushed against his guard trying to get clear; Camp converted. Seconds later Johnson took a wild shot off the Belmont backboard, and the Hornets scored a quick break. The home team led 49-48.

Denton hustled Craig and Eddie back onto the court. Six minutes left.

"Let me have another crack at 'em," begged Frank.

"We'll see," parried Denton.

He wasn't so sure Hurst would go back in. Hampton seemed to know just what to do about the defensive weaknesses of a line-up which had Frank and Perry at forwards, Sledge at center, Jamie and Buster at guards. They could gang Crickett in the keyhole and score by sheer numbers. Even if Craig stood only six-three, he was the one Belmont player who could handle Hampton's height.

Craig worked the ball in to Moss. He was their hope with two Hornets guarding Sledge. Eddie sank the basket which put the Blues ahead again. But the lead changed five times in the next four

177

minutes. The score stood 59-58 with 120 seconds left. Denton sent in the eager Hurst. Moss just couldn't get through to the basket. If Frank could hit one or two fallaway shots quickly—

He hit one. Belmont led 60-59. But Mutt Camp broke away from Frank and dribbled in for the layup which gave Hampton a single point's edge again.

Sixty-five seconds left! The Hampton gymnasium was bedlam. Slowly Craig dribbled upcourt. He pitched the ball to Buster and called out something. The towhead nodded and lobbed to Perry in the corner. Out came the ball to Craig. These were deliberate passes. The second hand was well on its last swing. Forty-five seconds, thirty! Denton stood up, as excited as any other onlooker. Townsend's intent was plain. Belmont would wait a few more seconds, then risk victory on one basket try. Why not? thought Denton. Frank Hurst was in there, straining, gesturing for the ball. Why not trust Hurst for one crucial basket? Was there a better shot in junior-college basketball? This Townsend, gloated Denton, thought of everything.

Twenty seconds—fifteen. Back and forth flew the ball between Buster and Craig. Now, boys, whispered Denton. *Right now!*

Then came the bold Belmont bid. Craig wheeled

toward Frank—but he whirled off with the ball. Townsend evaded one lunging Hornet guard. He pivoted sharply and went up high and—

His hook shot was good! Somehow it had cleared Greer's flailing hands. Belmont led 61-60 with nine seconds left! And led by virtue of as clever a basket drive as Coach Denton had ever seen.

A desperate long shot failed for Hampton, and the game was over.

Chapter Eleven

The Belmont sports writer went overboard on Craig's field goal in the final seconds. "They took the wraps off the Pressure Kid Tuesday night, and lean Craig Townsend exploded like a comet to score the field goal which meant victory for Belmont's Blue Wave . . ."

Coach Denton smiled. It had been a fine play, taking the desperate Hampton defense by surprise and the coach, also. He had been sure that Craig meant to pass in to Frank for the crucial basket try. But it was smart basketball, uncanny strategy. The Blues had never registered a bigger field goal in all Denton's experience as coach. If Belmont could eke out a repeat victory, the Blues would need only to split the Warmouth series to take the championship.

Hampton might be tougher or easier in this game; there was no way of knowing. The home court advantage might or might not be important. It hadn't hurt Belmont to open the series in the Hornet gymnasium. In fact, the Blue squad had played as well on the road all season as at home.

Anyhow, mused Denton, he would not change his team's pattern. He told Frank so. Hurst had asked for return to full-time duty.

"I can't change a winning game, son. I'll put you in and keep you in as long as you're hitting."

"Then let Townsend stay in with me," argued Frank. "I'll work with him—anything he says. Believe me, Coach, I want us to win this championship more than anything else."

"Even more than getting a Crownover bid?"

"Yes, sir," Hurst said spiritedly. "We can worry about that after the season is over."

"Well," said Denton slowly, "we'll give it a try."

He found it easy to believe in Frank's sincerity. He wasn't sure why, but he felt that Townsend didn't completely trust Frank. Probably, thought the coach, the lean playmaker was wary of such a basket hog. Certainly Frank's style contrasted with all Craig had learned from Gil Wayne.

Captain Gilbert Wayne! The letter from the former Eastern College coach excited Coach Denton. He read it eagerly, then reread it several times. Gil Wayne had penned four full pages about the young soldier he had developed into a star player. Some of Wayne's statements surprised Coach Denton; others did not. The Blue mentor carefully folded the letter into his billfold. What would he do about it? Confront Craig Townsend? He would if he must, decided Denton, but not unless he had to. The championship was the most important thing. If it could be won without any unpleasantness, then fine. But, resolved the Blue coach, it would not be lost with the entire squad not knowing how the legendary Gil Wayne felt about his protégé.

*　　*　　*　　*　　*

Hampton threw the same attack at Belmont. Greer, Camp, Hardy, and Johnson worked the boards hard. This foursome put the visitors off to a 15-8 lead before Denton put patches on his starting line-up. And Hurst turned out to be a very purple patch indeed. Never had Denton seen the black-haired forward respond so well to pressure. Frank recorded ten points in six hectic minutes, and Jamie Brooks sank two set shots from outside the circle. The score stood 22-21 in the Blues' favor when Denton decided Hurst's splurge was over.

Belmont's starting combination grimly guarded the four Hornet pointmakers. Moss came up with his most spirited play of the season. The officials seemed a little lax about calling body contacts, and Denton risked Barley at center for an interval, long enough to rest Sledge. Frank returned to action for another two minutes and passed off to Perry for two baskets. The Blue margin of 38-32 put Denton in a good humor as he followed his players to the dressing room.

He saw no point in disturbing this club with anything. Denton praised them as a group, and Frank in particular. "You're working, son. Those feeds to Perry were beauties."

"Let me play more," begged Hurst. "I'll feed. I swear it."

Denton nodded. He would do that. Hurst was playing team basketball finally, forgetting all about personal glory. He was lifting the team up, proving a real leader. Denton could look forward to this next half confidently. His club held a slight but obvious edge on the floor. Hampton's only chance was for its scoring quintet to start hitting most of its shots.

They couldn't do that—not with Craig moving from one to the other, Crickett stoutly guarding the keyhole, and Perry playing better than ever. Belmont led 48-39 when Frank took over for Eddie.

He was letting sentiment get the best of judgment, mused Denton. The situation didn't call for a change of strategy. The Blue combination was in charge. But the coach sympathized with the black-haired forward, especially since studying Gil Wayne's long letter about Craig Townsend.

Hurst didn't have his first-half touch. His shots either rolled off the rim or bounded out. And, with the Blue defense weakened, Hampton closed the gap. The count was 51-47 when Frank left the court.

Craig's favorite combine turned to ball control. It seemed early to stall, but Coach Denton did not interfere. Why shouldn't he trust this playmaker's judgment? Even Gil Wayne described him as never making a mistake. Except one, that is, thought Denton—a mistake which had nothing to do with the strategy of any particular game.

The Hornets pressed the Blue players harder. They couldn't help it. The seconds were racing by. Only four minutes were left. Craig and Buster drew most of the fouls as Hampton fought for the ball. Both were dead shots from the free throw mark. Their single-pointers matched the visitors' floor shots. With two minutes left Belmont led 58-53.

In went Jamie for the tiring Sledge. The Blues had five ball-handlers on the floor. Two of Hampton's rangy shooters fouled out in quick succession, and Coach Denton knew the game was won. He sent in replacements for Craig and Buster. The gymnasium shook with the home crowd's ovation for the lean Blue playmaker. Seconds later the game ended, and overjoyed Belmont fans swarmed the bench. Belmont 61, Hampton 56! Coach Denton heaved a sigh of relief. An even break with Warmouth would mean his first championship as Belmont coach.

✻   ✻   ✻   ✻   ✻

But the Warriors were tougher than the Hampton Hornets. Denton knew that after the first five minutes of action. Warmouth led 12-6 and deserved the margin. The Blue coach had not fully appreciated the Warrior center's ability. Ed McCabe towered six-ten and outmoved Sledge on both defense and offense. Craig quickly shifted onto the Warrior ace and fared some better. But McCabe just played more cautiously, resorting to hook shots rather than crips. He got off those shots despite Townsend's best efforts.

Denton sent in Hurst and Jamie, bringing Eddie and Buster to the side lines. The Blue coach didn't see how he could spare Craig even a minute or two, not the way this McCabe was racking up points.

He should have known this was coming, thought Denton. The Blue defense was facing an offensive it could not subdue. Warmouth's Chuck Everett was almost as deadly from the circle as was McCabe in the keyhole. How had Hampton split its series with this sure-shooting Orange team? By outscoring it, of course. By matching one dizzy offense against another. And Belmont didn't have a high-powered attack, especially not with Sledge so well covered.

Denton sighed and shifted around in his chair. Did everything depend on Frank's showing? The coach saw no other hope. Crickett had plainly met his match. And why expect Eddie to suddenly emerge as a sensational pointmaker? He was largely to blame himself, reflected the coach. He'd let his plan to develop a third backboard threat be side-tracked. It had been too easy to settle for Craig Townsend's type of basketball, which had produced quick results.

Hurst scored immediately. The black-haired forward broke across the circle, with Crickett an unintentional screen. Townsend fed Frank the ball. Up went Hurst for his left-handed fallaway. The ball swished through the netting, and Belmont trailed 12-8.

Downcourt raced the Orange quintet. Jim Maddox to Chuck Everett; he faked a shot and flipped in to McCabe. The Warrior center leaped and stretched, but Townsend was high, too. McCabe flicked the ball back to Everett and screened the Orange marksman's shot. A two-pointer. Jamie passed to Craig, off to Hurst. The veteran whirled, but Everett had him covered. Frank spun around, and Maddox almost slapped the ball free. Hurst managed to pass in to Crickett, but McCabe covered this threat. Back went the ball to Craig. Jamie Brooks eventually tried a long one-hander. It rolled off, and Maddox cleared the board. In to McCabe, up on the rim—the hook shot was good. Warmouth 16, Belmont 8.

Denton gestured for his players to ask for time out. "We must get more points," he told them. "Shoot more and shoot quicker."

Craig shook his head. "We'll just lose the ball."

"This way," snapped Denton, "we're just losing the game. The championship, too. If we can't hold 'em at home, what chance do we have in their gym?" He strode back to the bench. He meant what he had said. He was ready to send in Buster Tolar if playmaker Townsend didn't carry out instructions.

Craig obeyed. In fact, he made it obvious that he was carrying out orders to the letter. He fed Hurst recklessly, and the veteran forward quickly adapted his shooting to the changed tempo. For the next eight minutes Belmont matched Warmouth shot for shot. The 12-point difference was the result of the Warriors' better shooting. Warmouth 30, Belmont 18!

Coach Denton tried another experiment. Eddie Moss returned to forward, and Buster resumed his guard duties. Eddie tallied twice in the next minute and a half. The only way to beat this Orange team, decided Denton, was to outscramble them on the boards. The coach's eyes hardened as he watched Townsend go high to foil McCabe's hook shot. Belmont had the other man to send up on the rim. He didn't want to go. He was determined to be a playmaker. He was convinced such a role promised a better individual return. He played for that and that alone. What happened in the keyhole and around the hoop wasn't his business. Why should he worry about it? Didn't he play his guard position almost perfectly? Didn't he show up better than his teammates when the score went against the Blues?

Of course Townsend did. Denton looked up at the clock. Three minutes and ten seconds left. Well, Craig Townsend had exactly that long to go as Belmont's backcourt director! Forrest Denton had made up his mind. Jamie and Perry would man the guard posts the next half. Crickett would play center as usual. But the Blue forward assignments would be changed. Frank Hurst would return to full-time duty. Eddie Moss would round out the line-up—unless one Craig Townsend had a sudden and complete change of heart. Denton doubted that would happen. Hadn't Townsend successfully defied the grimmest taskmaster ever to coach college basketball? Gil Wayne had stated so in his letter to Forrest Denton. "Frankly, I was glad when Townsend was discharged. I taught him a great deal in a short time, but I was never able to handle him. He was his own man from start to finish. Except for this one quality, I could have developed him into the finest all-around player I ever knew. He may turn out to be that anyhow. But I predict that your team will be defeated while he proves it."

❀　❀　❀　❀　❀

They couldn't see the scoreboard from the Belmont dressing room, but everyone knew what it showed. Warmouth's half-time lead of 46-31 appeared insurmountable. Frank Hurst wasn't the only miserable Blue player.

"I can't figure it out," groaned Hurst. "They're giving us a good country licking."

"They sure are," agreed Coach Denton. He held

up his hand for silence. "And I'll explain why." He looked at Craig, and his eyes glinted. "Or do you want to tell them, Townsend?"

"Tell them what?"

"Tell them why you won't shift to forward and team with Sledge on the boards," Denton answered coldly. "Tell them you're proving your worth as a playmaker to Crownover and professional scouts. Tell them you realize you'll never be an All-American post man; you're just not tall enough. You know big-time basketball won't be much impressed by the points a six-three player scores in junior college. But Crownover or any other school will go for a crack six-three playmaker."

Denton licked his lips. "So you won't go into the keyhole," the coach continued. "You're a smart feeder and assist man, and you can prove it. You want everybody to realize it. So you won't feed a basket hog like Frank Hurst. You don't want him setting all kinds of scoring records and getting credit for the team's victories. You want him to score some—and Sledge some—and Moss a few. But you want to play ball control and a tight defense mainly. You're the whole show there."

Denton paused. Craig sat silent, tight-lipped, staring at the floor. "Am I wrong, Townsend?" demanded the coach. "Was Gil Wayne wrong, too?

He was glad to see you discharged, Townsend."
The coach took out Wayne's letter. "I have it here
in writing. And he refused to contact any of his
coaching friends in your behalf. You had to paddle
your own canoe. You didn't mind that so much.
You had saved your service pay. You found out
about the close ties between Crownover and Belmont. So you just registered here on your own and
came out for the team. You didn't show me any of
your clippings, Townsend. Why not?"

"I don't keep clippings," muttered Craig.

"Not even the one where you set a new one-game
scoring record in the All-Service Tournament? Why
is that, Townsend? You're not proud of scoring
forty-one points in a tournament game?"

"Look," Craig snapped, lifting his head. "Let's
get something straight. Did I ask you for any help
when I came here? Has Belmont helped me in any
way? Haven't I paid my own freight?" His eyes
swept his teammates. None answered him. "What
do I owe you characters?" he demanded. He looked
back to the coach. "You handed me a suit and
you've let me use a locker. Anything else? Not
that I know of. Now what do I owe you for the
suit? How much locker rent? How much for the
soap and water I've used in the showers? I'll pay

it—right now. Then I don't want to hear any more squawking about my owing anybody anything."

Coach Denton studied the aroused player a moment, then nodded. "You're right, Townsend," the mentor said softly. "Quite right. You've used us, and we've used you. That's all there is to a team the way you see it. We like to look at it in a different way. But we issued you a suit your way, and we'll settle up your way." The coach stood up. "We needed a playmaker," he said slowly. "You were it. We used you to get this far. Now that's not enough. We need a surprise package for the next half. For the next game, too, if we can't catch up in this one. We need to come up with a new threat on the boards. That's not your style. So we'll settle up right now. Keep the suit, Townsend. Maybe you don't think much of it now, but you'll value it as a souvenir someday. You'll get old enough after a while that souvenirs mean something."

Denton gestured with both hands. "The school won't mind the cost, Townsend. I think we would have retired your uniform. Hung it in a trophy case in the gym's lobby for all future Belmont hopefuls to see. You could have left the suit hanging there— and we would have put a sign or something to show who wore the uniform—and why we built a special trophy case for it. We would have written something like, 'Craig Townsend, Belmont's greatest all-around player.' People would have remembered you a long time as the playmaker who cut loose from the backcourt to win Belmont's first championship."

The coach shrugged his shoulders. "But that's *our* way of playing the game, Townsend, not yours. And it doesn't mean a thing."

"It does," Craig said tersely, "and you know it." He took a deep breath. "All right," he snapped. "Hurst and I will take forwards. Can you keep up, Frank? Can you forget about those fallaway shots and come in on the boards with me?"

"I can do anything you can," Hurst blazed back. "I'll feed you the ball; you put it in the basket."

Craig studied Hurst a moment, then turned to Denton. "Somebody will put it in," he said. A smile formed on his lean features. "Me at first," he added. "They won't be expecting that."

* * * * *

Fifteen points behind! Could any team overcome such a lead against strong competition? The Blue quintet immediately showed that it meant to try.

Sledge got the tip, no small feat itself against McCabe. He slapped the ball to Perry. Stanton threw to Craig at the top of the circle. The Warriors shifted quickly to cover both Hurst and Sledge. The former played his role better than Crickett. Frank cut across the keyhole as if expecting to take the ball. Craig feinted to him, then pivoted around a Warrior opponent to drive for the basket. His angled shot plopped into the netting.

Denton took a deep breath. Gil Wayne hadn't exaggerated. Nor had Eddie Moss and Crickett in describing Townsend's performance in their special practice sessions. Craig played a forward's position as if born to it. And Frank Hurst was working like a beaver to set up scoring opportunities for his running mate. Craig scored the basket which cut Warmouth's lead to 46-35. Then the troublesome Everett sank two successive baskets while the Blue offense bogged down temporarily. Townsend lost the ball trying to feed Sledge.

Hurst hit a fallaway, and Denton grinned happily. He did not want the black-haired letterman shelving his own scoring opportunities. Craig was a smooth hand working through the keyhole. Sledge went up for a successful hook and the count was 50-39. But Belmont needed Frank's deadly, unorthodox shooting. No one defensive player could smother those fallaways. Craig and Sledge must hit enough to compel the Warriors to use a standard defense.

Craig again, breaking away from his guard dribbling clear under the basket, hooking in his shot from outside the circle. McCabe laid in a rebound for Warmouth. Sledge fought up through a tangle of arms and bodies to roll in for a hook. The Belmont beanpole sank his free try and the count was 52-44.

Such an attack reduced the effectiveness of the Blues' defense. Craig was often too late to help against Warrior drives into the keyhole. McCabe soared up on the board for a two-pointer. But Hurst hit again almost immediately. Frank, Craig, Crickett—this trio wasted little time getting off their shots. Townsend strained backward and sank a two-handed jump. He leaped up and knocked in a rebound. Warmouth called a time out with the score 54-50. Belmont had gained ten points in as many minutes. Craig Townsend had registered five field goals.

Denton sent Eddie in. Frank needed a breathing spell. He did during every period; he couldn't hold his furious pace for more than eight or ten minutes. Frank sat on the side lines and shouted hoarse encouragement to his teammates.

They needed it. The Warriors were nowhere near

through. The visitors came out of their huddle with a furious scoring pattern which produced eight quick points while the Blue quintet was limited to a single field goal.

Warmouth had a surprise scoring package, too—Charlie Jameson. He tallied three of the baskets with breaks in from the corners.

Warriors 62, Belmont 52. Frank hurried in to his forward's position. Denton's eyes twinkled as he realized the visitors' defensive strategy. They were still convinced that Frank was the shooter to be stopped. Warmouth assigned only one guard to Craig, while McCabe played Sledge single-handed. Maddox, their defensive ace, covered Frank with an outside guard sliding over to watch for fallaways.

And that bothered Hurst not at all. He played heroically, drawing the Warrior defense to him with his feints, feeding off to Sledge or Townsend. Crickett was as quick to move on the ball. Craig could outfight his man under the basket, and his teammates kept him busy. The Warrior covering him fouled out with four minutes left. The score stood 70-65 then. Townsend had tallied most of those points. He had 21 to his credit already. He sank a jump shot from the circle to make the count 70-67.

Warmouth elected to slow down the game, but

Perry and Jamie were top hands against dribbling opponents. Perry slapped the ball downcourt to Frank. Up he went for his favorite shot, but before he got it off he realized Craig was charging in. Hurst flicked the ball off to Townsend, and he went up for his twenty-fifth point.

Everett dropped in a set shot. The Warriors gained the ball as Sledge missed a hook, but they chose not to stall. McCabe rolled in a leaping hook. Less than ninety seconds left.

Denton sent Buster in for the weary Perry. Craig was tired, too, near exhaustion, but he refused to leave the floor.

"We can take 'em," he panted, "but make Frank shoot, Coach. I'm not sure I have another drive in me."

Coach Denton had to smile despite the tense situation. Here was Townsend begging Frank Hurst to try for the basket. Sledge echoed the appeal. He had run out of steam, too.

Denton nodded. This idea suited him. Let the Blues get the ball, then leave the rest to Frank.

"Get it in somehow," he told the black-haired forward. "You can do it."

Could he—with two Warriors hanging onto him? Up he went, jerking backward, pumping the ball left-handed while twisting sideways. The ball rolled

197

around the rim, flopped through. Thirty-two seconds left, and Warmouth ahead 72-71.

The visitors meant to take no chances on losing the ball. Each pass was studied, deliberate. Buster, however, outguessed the Warrior guards. He slapped the ball free, and Craig screened Jamie's scramble. He came up with the wild ball and pitched back to Sledge before falling forward. Crickett threw to Craig. The lean playmaker charged the Warrior defense as if meaning to drive for the rim himself. But he flipped the ball off to Frank, and the black-haired forward leaped and twisted, pumping the ball with his left hand. It rolled around the hoop twice and then plunked through.

Ten seconds left. A blue-jerseyed player broke through the Warrior pattern and seized the ball. Hurst again. He held it triumphantly aloft as the gun sounded.

Forrest Denton rose slowly. For an instant he doubted that his legs would hold him. Then he steadied himself and started pushing toward the two finest players he had ever coached.

✿　✿　✿　✿　✿

That was what he told Coach Bart Millican of Crownover three nights later. Forrest Denton was not nearly so excited then. The Blue quintet had repeated its victory over Warmouth to finish unbeaten and untied. But the second win was an anticlimax. McCabe went out early with a wrenched ankle, and Sledge was never covered after that. He scored 34 points as the Blues won 78-66.

"But we won the championship Tuesday night," Denton reminded Millican. "Frank and Craig did it. I'd hate to choose between those two."

"So would I," agreed Herbert Petry. Millican, Denton, and Petry were waiting for Craig and Frank in the rich man's hotel suite. "I was all set to push Townsend, but then Frank showed us a great court game. Now—well, I just don't know."

Coach Millican smiled. "You two worry over nothing. I have already talked to both of them, or listened rather. Hurst tried to sell us on Townsend. Then Craig turned right around and tried to convince us we should take Hurst. So we are going to do the logical thing."

"What's that?" Mr. Petry asked eagerly.

"Why, take both," said Millican with a shrug. "The way they work together, who would want to separate them?"

"That's true," agreed Mr. Petry. He turned to Denton. "How did you get them working together,